The Ship of Adventure

Jack settled down to study the map intently, too engrossed to notice a huge shadow falling over him from the window opposite.

"AAAAGH!!!"

Letting out a terrible roar of triumph, Igor slammed his huge hands onto the glass, just centimetres from Jack's face.

He'd seen the map at last!

Terrified, Jack shot to his feet and made a run for it. Igor charged after him like an enraged bear.

Heart hammering, Jack raced through the door and along the empty deck. He clambered up some steel steps with Igor thundering after him, swiping at his legs from below. Jack raced on, up, up, as far as he could go, onto a stretch of deck – and stopped. There was no exit! Threateningly, Igor closed in on him . . .

*There are eight screenplay novelisations
starring Philip, Dinah, Jack and Lucy-Ann from the
Channel Five Enid Blyton™ Adventure Series:*

*All published by
HarperCollinsPublishers Ltd*

Enid Blyton's™

The Ship of
Adventure

Screenplay novelisation by
Alice McCann

Collins
An imprint of HarperCollinsPublishers

Original screenplay by
Charles Hodges.

This screenplay novelisation first published
in Great Britain by Collins 1997
1 3 5 7 9 10 8 6 4 2

Collins is an imprint of HarperCollins*Publishers* Ltd,
77-85 Fulham Palace Road, Hammersmith, London W6 8JB.

Copyright © Enid Blyton Ltd 1997

ISBN 0 00 675308 6

The author asserts the moral right to be
identified as the author of this work.

Printed and bound in Great Britain by
Caledonian International Book Manufacturing Ltd,
Glasgow, G64

Conditions of Sale
This book is sold subject to the condition that it shall not,
by way of trade or otherwise, be lent, re-sold, hired out or otherwise
circulated without the publisher's prior written consent in any form
of binding or cover other than that in which it is published and
without a similar condition including this condition being
imposed on the subsequent purchaser.

CHAPTER ONE

"Look at Kiki!" said Jack. The white parrot was stalking ahead of the children towards a group of gulls perched on the cliff edge.

"Careful, Kiki," laughed Dinah. "They're meaner than you!"

Kiki stalked on, head lowered. The gulls turned to stare at her. One began to shuffle in her direction. It lowered its head, too.

"Kiki – watch *out*!" shouted Jack, and with his shout the seabirds rose as one into the air, crying and calling. Kiki flew up too, circling with the gulls, until she lost her nerve and flapped back to Jack.

"Really, Kiki," said Jack, as he settled her back on his shoulder. "Whatever got into you? You're not a seagull."

"She only wanted an adventure," said Lucy-Ann, Jack's sister.

"Know how she feels," muttered Philip.

"Hey," said Bill, smiling, as he strode over to join the children. "That's enough of that kind of talk. We want *no* adventures of any kind for at least the next month. Now, let's finish this quiet, uneventful walk and go back to Craggy Tops for a quiet uneventful lunch, shall we?"

Bill Cunningham was an old friend who was getting married to Dinah and Philip's mother in a few days, time. His job at the Foreign Office, always very secret, meant that he was frequently involved in dangerous and exciting adventures.

Far away from Craggy Tops, in the middle of London, a long black limousine slowed to a halt in front of a museum. A huge man emerged and stamped up the grand marble steps to the entrance. He walked straight through the display halls, eyes down, oblivious to all the exhibits. Then he turned into a side room where small wooden models were kept.

A case in the centre of the room caught his attention. He stopped and stood grinning down at a beautiful model of a Roman galley ship, encased in a bottle. It was perfect in every tiny detail.

Suddenly the man gave a determined roar, raised a fist the size of a ham and smashed it into the glass case. As the alarms wailed around him he seized the model boat and charged towards an open window. Down the fire escape he clambered, his great bulk moving at amazing speed. He jumped the last two steps and ran towards the black limousine that was waiting silently below.

The smoked glass window of the back door slid down and a face looked out. It was a sinister face, smooth and evenly proportioned like a snake's. The hair, long, black and greasy, was tied in a pony-tail at the back of the man's neck. "Well, Igor?" came a hiss.

"Here, Boss. I got it," crowed the huge man.

Igor's boss seized the ship-in-a-bottle and disappeared into the darkness of the car. There, he dashed it against the back seat, smashing the glass. He shook off the splinters from the boat and cradled it in his hands for a moment. Then he greedily pulled open a tiny panel in its base. His fingers groped inside, urgently, desperately

– then, turning on Igor, he let out a terrifying snarl of disappointment.

"This isn't the one!" he hissed.

"But – Mr Slade, sir—"

"I said it's empty! There's nothing here!" Angrily, he thrust the boat into Igor's hands. "Now beat it! And take that junk with you!"

The window slid up and the limousine pulled away. Igor stood in the road, bewildered.

"Boss!" he wailed. "Don't just leave me here!" He dropped the boat onto the road and shambled after the retreating car.

The perfect little boat lay in the gutter, smashed and broken.

Meanwhile, Bill and the children had arrived back at Craggy Tops and now a fast and furious game of ball was taking place in the garden.

"Jack!" shouted Philip. "Here!"

Jack spun round and passed it to Philip who cried, "Lucy-Ann! Catch!" The ball flew overhead, and Bill jumped, too late.

"Hey!" he yelled. "Who's on my side?"

Lucy-Ann squealed with laughter as she threw the ball to Dinah.

"Not fair!" protested Bill. "I'm in a one-man team here!"

"Hey, you lot!" came a voice from a window above them. Everyone looked up and saw Alison Mannering, Dinah and Philip's mother, smiling down at them, her long blonde hair swinging over the sill. "Does anybody here know what tomorrow is?"

"Um," said Philip, grinning. "Saturday, isn't it, Mum?"

"Start of the weekend..." added Lucy-Ann.

"Day before Sunday..." put in Bill.

"But there *was* something else..." said Jack, "wasn't there, Bill?"

Bill screwed up his face in concentration. "Wait – wait – it's coming to me – it's – it's our wedding day!"

The children broke into loud cheering. No one was happier than they were that Alison and Bill had decided to get married. Alison smiled, and then folded her arms in mock severity. "All right, you lot," she said. "Joking's over. I want you all to try on your outfits before lunch."

"While they still fit, you mean," said Bill. "Come on, last one in gets extra spinach – hey – don't push!"

In the excitement, no one heard the mobile phone on the dashboard of Bill's open-topped car start to ring. No one but Kiki the parrot, that is. Kiki loved bells – any kind of bells. She flew onto the dashboard to investigate.

"Boys – upstairs with Bill," ordered Alison. "Girls – your outfits are in here."

Dinah and Lucy-Ann raced into the living room, followed by Alison. Their bridesmaids' outfits were laid out on a sofa. At top speed they stripped off and pulled on the flouncy green frocks.

"I feel like a queen!" sang Dinah as she danced about the room. "I love this *swish swish* sound!"

Lucy-Ann wobbled on the coffee table as Alison put a last few stitches in the hem of her skirt. "Do you mind very much about us going away?" asked Alison.

"No," assured Lucy-Ann. "Well – a bit."

Lucy-Ann and Jack didn't have a real home. Their parents were dead so until they met Dinah and Philip they had mostly lived with an aunt and uncle. Now, whenever they could, they stayed with the Mannerings.

"But when you come back," put in Dinah, swishing over to them, "we'll have a great dad. So it's worth waiting for."

"That's good," said Alison, smiling.

Jack was far less pleased with his wedding outfit than the girls were. He glared at his reflection in the mirror, his face as long as his trousers.

"Cheer up, Jack," said Bill. "I thought you were looking forward to this wedding?"

"I am," grumbled Jack. "But I hate this suit. And tomorrow night you're going off on your cruise to the Channel Islands. And we'll only have Uncle Joss to look after us and it's my birthday on Tuesday and Uncle Joss's cake tastes like—"

Uncle Joss was Dinah and Philip's great-uncle. He'd lived with the Mannerings for as long as they could remember. He now appeared beside Jack, saying, "What's this? What do I hear? Discontent in the ranks?"

"Jack thinks he looks silly in his wedding gear," said Philip hastily. He didn't want to hurt the old man's feelings repeating what Jack had really said. "He's right, too."

13

"Don't blame you, my boy," said Uncle Joss. "Do you know, there's a tribe on the island of Dingtak that used to go to weddings dressed only in banana skins held together with fish bones."

"'Used to', Uncle Joss?" asked Philip. "Why did they stop?"

"People kept slipping on the banana skins. The hospitals were overflowing."

"Oh, Joss," laughed Bill. Then he ducked as Kiki came swooping up the stairs. Bill still found it hard living with a bird that hardly ever used a cage.

"You'd like that, wouldn't you, Kiki?" said Jack. "Thousands of bananas to eat."

"Bananas, bananas," squawked Kiki, and flew back outside. She could hear the phone ringing again. She landed on the dashboard and walked over the "ON" button on the phone. The ringing stopped.

"Hello?" said a very grand-sounding voice. "Cunningham? It's Houghton here. Cunningham? Is that you?"

"Naughty boy!" squawked Kiki. "Naughty boy!"

CHAPTER TWO

"What do you actually do on a cruise?" asked Lucy-Ann, twirling round so that Alison could fix the big bow at the back of her dress.

"Well," answered Alison, "the ship we're going on has lots of things to do. Deck games, shows, you know. There's lots of lovely food to eat. And every day or so we stop off at an island and we can get off and explore."

"I think I'll go on a cruise on my honeymoon," said Lucy-Ann dreamily. "What about you, Dinah?"

"Nah," scoffed Dinah. "Too safe. I'm going to South America. Up the Amazon."

"There now," said Alison, giving the bow a pat. "What do you think of your dress?"

"It's beautiful," breathed Lucy-Ann. "I

can't wait."

"Well, it's not long to go—" Alison broke off as Kiki shot squawking past the window. Seconds later the bird returned, perched on the sill, and did an ear-splitting imitation of a siren.

"What's got into Kiki?" said Lucy-Ann.

In the car, the voice on the other end of the phone barked, "Cunningham? *Cunningham*! What on earth's going on? Oh, for goodness sake. I'll try again."

The phone went quiet, and then it rang once more. This time, Bill heard it. He strode from the front door to his car, and picked it up.

"Cunningham here," he announced, then his face set in a rigid frown as he rapped out, *"What??!!* You must be joking." There was a short pause, then Bill barked: "This is absolutely ridiculous! It's out of the question! You must see that!"

Jack, Philip and Uncle Joss arrived at the front door together and peered out. "Bill seems a bit rattled," murmured Philip.

"Maybe it's nothing," answered Jack. "Maybe it's wedding nerves."

But Bill was still speaking furiously into the phone, arguing with someone. It certainly didn't sound like nothing.

"What's going on?" called out Alison anxiously.

"I don't know," answered Philip. "Bill sort of exploded."

"Saw that happen once to a fellow in Karaganda," put in Uncle Joss. "Turned out he'd eaten a month's ration of chillies at one sitting."

"Oh, charming," said Alison.

And then they heard Bill shout, "Look, I must strenuously object. This is absolutely *outrageous*!"

A long, long silence followed. Somehow it was more alarming than the shouting.

At last, Bill came through the door. He looked stricken. "Bad news, I'm afraid," he said. "I've got to leave."

"But what about the wedding?" squealed Dinah.

Miserably, Bill looked at Alison. "We'll have to postpone it. I can't tell you how sorry I am. I've got to leave – tonight."

Ten minutes later, Alison and Bill were still rowing in the hall. Kiki flew from floor to ceiling and back again, crying, "Stop the noise!" The children crouched miserably

17

on the landing, peering down through the banisters. If Bill and Alison kept this fighting up there might never be a wedding at all.

"Believe me, Allie," said Bill. "I have no choice."

"But tomorrow of all days! What's so special about *this* job?"

"Sir George says—"

"Sir George! If I could get my hands on him—"

"It's a top-secret job, a very particular job—"

"I knew what I was letting myself in for – but the day before our wedding!"

"You and the kids come first, Allie. You know that. And if I could change it, I would. But—"

"It's not fair," muttered Dinah. "How can they make Bill go away just like that?"

"It's all part of the job," answered Jack. "If there's an emergency, he has to go. It's people like him who protect the rest of us."

"That's true, lad," said Uncle Joss, who had quietly joined them. "We owe a lot to people like him."

"Did this ever happen when Dad was alive?" asked Philip. Philip and Dinah's father had worked for the Foreign Office, too, before he died.

"All the time," said Uncle Joss. "Your poor mum even had to come home early from her honeymoon. But at least they managed to get married."

"This must be something really serious then," muttered Philip.

"And dangerous, too," whispered Lucy-Ann fearfully.

"Yes," said Uncle Joss, patting her hand. "Yes, I'm afraid it must."

Early that evening, Bill arrived at Sir George Houghton's office, glowering furiously.

"It's very good of you to come in like this, Cunningham," said Sir George breezily.

"Yes, it is," snapped Bill, ice-cold. "*Very* good."

"Well, the fact is, something very serious has come up—"

"And I'm the only person who can deal with it?"

"Yes," replied Sir George firmly. "Yes, as a matter of fact I believe you are. Kindly hear me out – perhaps then you'll understand. We think a gang of international gangsters is planning to furnish the guns to overthrow the government of Zimbawa. Now, believe me, Cunningham, I am deeply sorry about the interruption to your wedding. But this situation is urgent. These gangsters have to be stopped – before it's too late."

Bill frowned, grimly. He could see now why Sir George had called him in. "A scheme like that will cost a huge amount of money," he said. "Just where do they plan to get it from?"

"Where indeed! We think the villains are onto something that could make them a fortune – far more than they get from their usual crimes. What exactly they're onto we're not sure – but it's vital that we stop them getting their hands on this money."

"That's a pretty tall order, sir."

"I know. But we have one firm lead. We think we know the identity of the gangster in charge of the money-making scheme. If we can catch him, the whole rotten plan will fall apart."

Sir George opened a grey file and extracted a photograph, which he handed to Bill. Staring out at Bill was a sinister looking man with long black greasy hair, tied in a pony-tail at the nape of his neck.

"His name's Leon Slade," said Sir George, grimly. "He poses as a businessman, but he's one of the most evil men who's ever lived."

CHAPTER THREE

Halfway across the world, hidden behind
tall trees and locked iron gates, lay Slade's
luxurious headquarters. Inside, Igor
trembled under the tirade of anger from his
boss.

"It won't happen again, Boss, promise!"
he whimpered.

"And how do you propose keeping your
promise?" hissed Slade.

"We've located another three of those
model ships. It's got to be in one of them."

"But you said it *had* to be in that last one!
Why should I believe you this time?"

"Please, Boss! It's got to be in one of
them."

Slade moved in close to Igor. "I hope
you're right," he murmured. "For your
sake, I hope you're right. Do you
understand what I'm telling you?" And he

made a deadly gesture with his curved hand towards Igor's neck, like a scorpion about to strike.

Sweat broke out on Igor's brow as he backed away. "Y-yes, Boss," he stammered. "You're a very generous man."

"Just make sure you bring the boat to me," Slade rapped out. "The *right* boat."

In the living room at Craggy Tops, Alison sat sadly putting her cruise tickets into an envelope. Then she stood up and wandered out to the kitchen. The children, gloomily playing a board game in the corner, watched her go.

"At least Allie will be here for my birthday," said Jack.

"Jack, how can you be so selfish?" cried Dinah. "She was really looking forward to that cruise."

"Well, there's nothing to stop her still going," said Philip, suddenly.

"Don't be dim," Dinah snapped. "Why would she want to go on her own?"

"Not on her own," answered Philip. "With us."

*

It took only two seconds for the other three children to recognise the excellence of Philip's plan and seek out Alison in the kitchen. But as she listened Alison's face set into the expression they knew so well, the face that showed she'd made up her mind about something and would stand for no arguments.

"I mean – it would be great, Mum," Philip tailed off. "I mean – are there any reasons why we shouldn't all go?"

"Yes, there are," retorted Alison. "There are three very good reasons. One, the expense. Two, it means changing all the arrangements I've made for you—"

"Oh, *Mum*," moaned Dinah.

"And three, it means leaving Uncle Joss here on his own."

The children sighed, defeated. Alison stalked to the door. Then she turned back, a broad grin on her face. "But apart from that, the idea's brilliant," she cried. "I'll call the travel agent to check that there's room. You go and pack for the Channel Islands!"

And, whooping and cheering, that's just what the four did.

Alison was very subdued over breakfast

the next morning. The children knew she was thinking about the wedding that should have been taking place, and worrying about Bill and the danger he might be in. They tried to be extra kind to her all day as they finished their packing for the cruise.

At five o'clock Uncle Joss drove the five of them to the port where their cruise liner, *Aratika*, was berthed. At the sight of the majestic ship even Alison cried out with excitement. Dinah, determined to record the whole trip with her new camera, started snapping away from the minute they all got out of the car.

"I don't believe it," Philip breathed, as they walked up the broad gangplank. "One minute we're facing the most boring fortnight in history, the next we're here. How did we do it?"

"I don't know," laughed Jack, "and I don't care. Let's go and find our cabin!"

Inside the boys' cabin, Kiki hopped from Jack's shoulder and flew from chair to bed and back again, calling excitedly.

"Now you behave yourself on this trip, Kiki," said Jack sternly. "No siren noises in the night and so on. I promised the captain that he wouldn't even know you're here."

A blast from the foghorn and the sound of engines told the boys they had set sail, and they dashed to the porthole to look out. Water churned, seagulls wheeled above – yes, they were off!

Dinah poked her head round the door and said, bossily, "Come on, you two. Stop admiring the view. Haven't you even unpacked yet? We want to explore!"

In high spirits, the four children swayed and staggered down the corridors. They were still acquiring their sea-legs! The first port of call was the dining room. Inside, setting the tables, was a lively-looking young woman with a long brown ponytail.

She looked up and smiled at the four as they came in. "Hello, you lot," she said. "Are you hungry? Dinner won't be for another hour, I'm afraid."

Dinah laughed. "We're fine," she said. "We're just finding out about the ship."

"Well, I'm Ingrid. Who are you?"

"I'm Dinah, and this is my brother Philip –"

"And I'm Jack and this is my sister Lucy-Ann."

26

"Pleased to meet you all," said Ingrid. "Which cabins are you in?"

"101 and 102," said Jack.

"Oh, I'm your stewardess then! That's good. Aren't you the family with the bird?"

"Yes," answered Jack. "Her name's Kiki. She's a parrot."

"Well, I look forward to meeting her, too," said Ingrid, then she smiled jokingly as she saw Dinah train her camera on her.

"That's pretty," said Dinah, lowering her camera again and pointing to the oblong of engraved silver hung round Ingrid's neck.

"Thank you. It's the family heirloom – that's ancient runic writing."

The children were admiring the silver necklace when Alison walked in. "There you are!" she cried.

"This is Ingrid, Mum," said Dinah. "She's our stewardess."

"Pleased to meet you," said Ingrid.

"I'm Allie Mannering," said Alison warmly, as they shook hands. "Have they been bothering you?"

"Not at all," replied Ingrid. "Are these all your children?"

Alison grinned. "I suppose you could

say that."

"We're all together," said Philip.

The children laughed. Ever since the Mannerings had met Jack and Lucy-Ann they'd spent so much time together they considered themselves to be one family.

"Come on," said Alison. "Ingrid's got her work to do and you've got to finish your unpacking."

The children said goodbye and wandered back to their cabins. Not only was the ship absolutely brilliant, but their stewardess was great!

As the voyage got under way, the children explored the whole ship. When they got tired of exploring, they played deck games. They climbed ropes. They clambered into lifeboats and were chased out by a steward. They ate glorious food chosen from long menus at every meal, and threw what they couldn't eat over the sides for the flocks of screaming gulls.

Kiki shared in the luxury too – she dined royally on fat cherries saved from the children's ice-cream sundaes.

Even going to bed was fun on the ship. They would snuggle down into their crisp sheets and let the rhythmic swishing of the water below their portholes send them happily off to sleep. They had no inkling of the drama that was about to break about them!

CHAPTER FOUR

The next morning, at Leon Slade's headquarters, an expensive-looking Cadillac purred to a halt and a tall, confident Texan stepped out, carrying a long parcel wrapped in brown paper. Igor showed him to the dining room, where Slade was eating breakfast, and shut the door. Then Igor crouched down to listen at the keyhole. First he heard the sound of ripping paper – then the splintering of glass. He was only just in time to get out of the way as the door was flung open and the Texan hurtled through it.

"Fool!" spat Slade, after his fleeing form. "You know the penalty for failure." Then he turned menacingly on Igor...

Back in London, life was not nearly so rosy as it was on the cruise. Bill had stayed up all night in Sir George's office studying reports of recent crimes and had come up with nothing that seemed to be connected to Leon Slade. He was dozing uncomfortably on the plush sofa when Sir George walked in and cleared his throat pointedly. Poor Bill woke with a start.

"Here is today's Interpol report," announced Sir George. "All the thefts committed in the last twenty-four hours. I've glanced through it and I must say I can't see anything that would bring in the kind of money that those scoundrels need. Maybe you'll have better luck."

"I hope so," said Bill, tiredly, and began reading. As his eyes scanned the list something caught his attention. He grabbed a yellow highlighter and scored through the words: STOLEN: 12TH CENTURY REPLICA ROMAN GALLEY – HOUSTON, TEXAS.

It tied in with something he'd noticed on yesterday's list – a Roman galley stolen from London two days earlier. Why would anyone steal those old replica ships? You'd never be able to sell them – they were too easily traceable. He swivelled round to his computer console and tapped in an entry.

Soon, he was on the phone to an eminent professor of Ancient History at Cambridge University.

"...one in London, one in Houston, one in Cairo, and another never located. Thank you for your help, Professor."

Bill replaced the receiver and pressed his intercom. "Get me Cairo Museum," he said. He hoped he wasn't too late.

But that same day at Leon Slade's headquarters, another smashed model ship lay on the floor amid the splinters of its glass bottle, and a gentleman in sandals and Arabian head-dress was being flung out through the front door.

Igor trembled as his boss rounded on him.

"You *fool*," Slade spat, flexing his sinewy hands. "You know the penalty for failure!"

"Yes, Boss," muttered Igor. "Sorry, Boss. Next time—"

"Next time! What makes you think there will *be* a next time?"

"Please, Boss," Igor whimpered.

"You've got one more chance, Igor – one more."

"Sure, Boss," quaked Igor. "No sweat."

"And this time," hissed Slade, "I'm going with you."

CHAPTER FIVE

The *Aratika* sailed majestically on. After reading on deck for a while, Lucy-Ann decided she wanted a game of volley ball, and went looking for Dinah. She found her crouched on the floor of their cabin, wrapping up a glossy-looking book on computers.

"What's that?" asked Lucy-Ann.

"Jack's birthday present," replied Dinah, through a mouthful of Sellotape.

"Oh *no*," said Lucy-Ann.

"You haven't forgotten it, have you?"

"Yes! Completely! What am I going to do?"

"Grab your wallet and come with me."

Five minutes later they were in the ship souvenir shop. It wasn't very inspiring. It had shelves full of fluffy toys and posh bath salts with bows on, but nothing Jack would like.

"It's the same old stuff you buy everywhere," grumbled Lucy-Ann. "Oh – hi, Ingrid."

The friendly stewardess smiled at them. "Hi, you two," she said. "Spending all your money?"

"There's nothing to spend it on," said Lucy-Ann.

"It's Jack's birthday tomorrow," explained Dinah, "but she can't find anything he'd like."

"He likes computers," began Lucy, "and parrots and—"

"D'you think he'd like something to do with the sea and sailing?" interrupted Ingrid. "Something to remind him of this trip?"

"Hey – that's an idea. I'd like to get him something different."

"Well, tomorrow, where we stop, there's a wonderful nautical curiosity shop. I used to love going there when I was a little girl. I think it's still there."

As soon as the boat docked the next day, Dinah and Lucy rushed off to find the shop

35

Ingrid had described. And sure enough, just off the main square, there it was. The window alone was worth the trek. It was packed with ships' flags, shells, stuffed fish, anchors, telescopes, sea chests – everything you could think of to do with the ocean. Dinah immediately put her camera to her eye and snapped the wonderful display.

"Come on," said Lucy-Ann eagerly. "Let's go in!"

They tumbled through the tiny door of the shop and began gazing eagerly about them at all the shelves, groaning with yet more nautical goods.

"This is brilliant," said Dinah. "D'you think Jack would like this sailor's hat?" She tried it on.

"Maybe. What about that old deep-sea diving suit?"

"Oh, *yes*!" breathed Dinah. "I think want it!"

"Just a minute," said Lucy-Ann, as she paused in front of a small Roman galley in a glass bottle. "This is beautiful." She stooped and read the price tag. "And I can afford it – just!"

"It's perfect," said Dinah. "He'll love it."

Lucy-Ann paid the assistant, who wrapped up the ship-in-a-bottle carefully and put it in a sturdy paper bag. Then the girls piled out into the street, chatting happily, where they met up with Alison and the boys.

"Come on, now we're all together, group photo!" cried Dinah.

As the four posed, laughing, Slade and Igor walked behind them, just as Dinah clicked the shutter.

"Oh, bother," she said crossly. "That's ruined it. I didn't see them coming."

"Never mind," said Alison. "Time to get back to the ship."

"What have you got in that bag, Jack?" asked Lucy.

"Food for Kiki," said Jack. "What have you got in *your* bag?"

"That's for me to know and you to find out," retorted Lucy-Ann, smugly.

Minutes later, Slade and Igor stopped outside the nautical curiosity shop.

"Boss, it's gotta be the one," Igor was pleading. "If there was another one we would have heard about it."

"It's your neck, Igor," growled Slade.

37

Igor fingered his throat nervously as they went into the shop.

Igor's howl of anguish shook the windows of the shop and terrified the shop assistant when he heard her news. "You've just SOLD it?" he roared.

Slade leant over the counter, and seized the shop assistant by the arm. "*Who to?*" he hissed.

Alison and the children were too busy choosing ice-creams at a pavement café to notice Slade and Igor frog-marching the hapless shop assistant along the pavement, or to see the shop assistant point at Dinah and Lucy-Ann and beat a hasty retreat.

"You imbecile!" Slade snarled. "You useless, idiotic, cretinous imbecile! You should have reserved it!"

"It's OK, Boss," said Igor. "I can handle it now." And he reached inside his jacket.

Slade lunged at Igor's neck, hand flexed. "Don't be *stupid*," he spat. "Not in broad daylight! Now listen carefully!"

Oblivious, Alison and the children had started to walk back to the docks, finishing their ice-creams.

"Can we stay up really late tonight?"

Jack was saying. "It *is* my birthday."

"Go on, Mum!" urged Dinah.

"Presents at supper and then stay up as late as we want?"

"Like till two in the morning?" put in Philip.

"Certainly not!" laughed Alison – then gasped as Igor suddenly lurched in front of them. He collapsed on the ground clutching his chest, groaning horribly.

"Oh, my goodness!" exclaimed Alison. "Quick, Philip – loosen his collar!"

Dropping their purchases, everyone sprang to help. Philip unbuttoned Igor's collar. Jack lifted Igor's huge head from the pavement as Alison took his pulse.

"Oh, what's the matter with him?" wailed Dinah.

"I don't know," muttered Alison. She bent close to Igor's head. "Listen – can you hear me?"

Igor's eyes swivelled round and fixed on Slade's hand, as it appeared from a shop doorway and grabbed a cylinder-shaped paper bag from the pavement. Immediately, Igor started to heave himself onto his feet.

"Should I call an ambulance?" Dinah

said. "Hey – *wait*!"

But Igor was already staggering away.

"Stop!" cried Alison, putting a hand on his arm. "Wait a minute—"

"Get out of it!" grunted Igor, pushing her aside.

"Look," tried Alison once more, "you're not well! You need a doctor!"

But Igor had stumbled off, leaving them all dumbfounded.

Safe inside the white limousine, parked on the dock, Slade laughed greedily as he ripped away the paper bag from the package he'd stolen. "At last!" he crowed. "At—" His face fell. Inside the bag was a large tube of bird seed.

Igor was so confused that his brain, over-stretched even in the normal course of things, stopped working completely. "Boss? I didn't know you were getting a bird?"

"You *fool*!" shrieked Slade, slamming the bird seed into Igor's lap. He looked desperately out of the window, just in time to see Alison and the children walk through the harbour gates.

"After them!" he yelled. And the limousine pulled away.

"Who do you think he was?" asked Dinah, as they all made their way up the gangplank of the *Aratika*.

"Well, I did wonder if he'd been trying to trick us – but we haven't lost anything, have we?"

"No," said Lucy-Ann. "*I* certainly haven't." And she tucked the bag with the model boat in firmly under her arm.

"Oh, drat," said Jack, suddenly. "I left behind the parrot seed I bought for Kiki."

"Oh, she'll be fine," said Alison. "There's plenty of fruit and nuts on board."

As they all bustled aboard, nobody noticed the great shambling shape watching them from the dock. They didn't see him climb up the gangplank, pick up a crate of drinks and follow Lucy-Ann to the gift shop, where she bought some paper to wrap Jack's boat in. And they didn't see him follow her closer and closer to her cabin—

"Hello, Lucy-Ann!" said Ingrid cheerfully, appearing out of a doorway.

"Ingrid! Hi! That was a great shop you told us about!"

"It's good, isn't it?" agreed Ingrid,

turning away and nearly walking smack into Igor. "Ah, drink crates. I think you're lost. I'll show you the way to the store room. Follow me."

Igor tried to shuffle past her, but Ingrid raised her voice to repeat, *"Follow me!"*

And as Lucy-Ann safely shut the cabin door behind her, Igor had to obey.

CHAPTER SIX

"Big blow!" said Alison. Jack leant forward and blew out all the candles on his cake. Everyone cheered.

"Make a wish, make a wish!" cried Alison, as Jack closed his eyes tight.

"What have you wished for, Jack?" said Lucy-Ann teasingly. "That you get the biggest bit?"

Everyone laughed. In the corner of the ship's lounge, someone else was laughing too, enjoying the happy scene. It was Igor. He suddenly coughed, embarrassed, as though he'd remembered something, and hid himself behind his paper again.

Dinah picked up Jack's new tennis bat. "You've had some great presents," she said.

"I still don't understand this thing that Bill's given you, though," said Alison.

43

"It's a scanner," answered Jack. "Philip, pass me that book. Look, Aunt Allie. If I run it over this picture, I can transfer the image straight into my computer."

Alison was impressed. "Crikey! So it's a camera?"

"Sort of. It builds up a bit-map which the computer can understand."

"Unlike Mum!" put in Philip, and everyone laughed.

"Thank you very much, Philip!" retorted Alison. "Anyway, I like the ship-in-a-bottle best."

"So do I," said Jack, as he picked it up and turned it about in his hands, admiring it. "You're a star, Lucy-Ann."

Across the room, Igor peered round his paper, his eyes narrowing with greed.

"Hey," said Jack, as he examined the ship closely, "there's a name on it, with funny writing."

"Let's see," said Dinah, leaning over. "It's like the writing on Ingrid's pendant. She might know what it means – let's ask her. Can we, Mum?"

"All right," said Alison, "go on – but don't be long, or I'll eat all this cake myself!"

Laughing, the children scrambled out of the salon, Jack carrying the boat. Nobody noticed the bulky figure of Igor slipping out after them.

They found Ingrid setting the tables for the evening meal in the restaurant. She was only too happy to take a break and look at the boat.

"Hmm. Yes, it's certainly runic writing. I know a little bit about runes. I think it says 'Andrea'. That's a very special name."

"Why?" asked Jack.

"It's from a famous story. About a powerful Roman, in fact the Governor of these islands. He was a very greedy man, always stealing from the people."

"What did he do?" said Dinah.

"Well, he had a daughter, Andrea. An only child."

The children leaned closer to listen. Jack put the boat on a nearby chair.

Unnoticed, Igor crept into the dining room.

"And when she was going to be married," Ingrid continued, "the Roman said that all the silver in the country must be given to him to be melted down into coinage for her wedding."

Still unnoticed, Igor had managed to manœuvre his huge bulk under a nearby table.

"*All* the silver?" exclaimed Dinah.

"Every last little bit. He sent it on a ship to his daughter. The ship was called the *Andrea* as well. But en route it was attacked by pirates."

Pirates! The children gasped happily and drew closer still. No one spotted the hoover nozzle that was slowly snaking its way towards the chair with Jack's boat on.

"Did they get the silver?" asked Lucy-Ann.

"No," said Ingrid. "The story goes that the pirates chased the ship around an island – but no one knows where. And the captain was clever. He got away and went into a little harbour where he left the silver with some men. And then he came out to fight."

Behind the group, the hoover nozzle had hooked the chair safely and was pulling it slowly and steadily towards the table under which Igor was crouched.

"And who won?" asked Philip.

"Well – no one. Both the ships sank and

they all drowned."

"How awful!" exclaimed Lucy-Ann.

"And the treasure went missing," said Philip. "It must have been worth a fortune."

"Millions," replied Ingrid. "There's nothing you couldn't buy with it."

There was a moment's silence, then Dinah asked: "But is it *true*?"

"Who knows?" answered Ingrid, smiling. "But if it *is*, no one has ever found it."

Two hands the size of hams stretched from under the tablecloth towards the boat, stretched and reached –

"*Right!*" said Alison, sweeping into the room and sweeping up the boat, "I think it's time you lot went to bed."

There was a chorus of groans as Alison hustled the children from the room. But it was nothing compared to the groan Igor let out when his hands closed on emptiness!

CHAPTER SEVEN

A couple of hours later, the *Aratika* was sailing calmly on through the night, and the children were tucked up in bed. Alison sat up in her cabin bed, making a goodnight call to Uncle Joss.

"Oh, we're having a lovely time," she was saying. "Don't you worry about us. Now you make sure you—"

Alison broke off abruptly. Someone in the corridor outside had tried the handle of her cabin.

" – take care of yourself, Uncle Joss," she finished hurriedly. "Must go now. 'Bye!"

She replaced the receiver and stood up. "If you kids are wandering about –" she called out, warningly, as she pulled open the cabin door.

There was no one there. Alison stepped into the corridor and looked up and down.

It was deserted. She crossed over to the girls' cabin and peeped round the door; Dinah and Lucy-Ann were fast asleep. Satisfied, Alison closed their door quietly and tiptoed over to the boys' cabin. She opened the door and peered round. All she could see was the two boys, peacefully asleep, and the dim shape of Jack's ship-in-a-bottle on the table between the beds.

Alison smiled ruefully. "I take it all back," she murmured, tiptoeing from the room and pulling the door shut behind her.

As the door pulled away from him, Igor grinned in relief. He'd thought his time was up when that blonde woman had opened the door, but she hadn't seen him standing behind it. He aimed his torch straight at the model ship and, chuckling, crept between the two beds and picked the bottle up.

"*AAAAAAAAAGH!!*" he bellowed.

A small feathered demon, all beak and claws, had flown at him. He beat out at it, trying to protect his face, and dropped the bottle. It smashed on the floor.

"*Naughty boy! Naughty boy!*" shrieked Kiki.

In a complete panic, Igor fled!

Startled out of sleep, Jack sat bolt upright in bed just as the door slammed behind Igor.

"What's happened, Kiki?" he cried, his heart hammering. The bird fluttered excitedly to land on his shoulder, crying "*No, noo – oo!*"

Jack reached over and snapped on the bedside light. Philip groaned and sat up, rubbing sleep out of his eyes.

"What's up?" he mumbled.

"My ship!" wailed Jack.

Dumbly, the two boys stared down at all the broken glass on the floor and the model galley lying in the midst of it.

"What happened?" said Philip.

"Someone was here!" Jack said, hoarsely. "There was a man – he broke my ship—"

"Don't be daft," replied Philip, calmly. "It was Kiki, she knocked it over."

Suddenly the door was wrenched open and the silhouette of Alison appeared, hands on hips. "I thought it was too good to be true," she snapped. "What on earth are you two up to?" She started to walk towards them.

"Mind the glass!" cried Jack.

"It's all right, Mum, we'll clear it up,"

said Philip. "Kiki knocked over the bottle, that's all."

"Honestly, that bird," grumbled Alison. "Just make sure you don't cut yourselves, all right?"

She turned on her heels just as Dinah and Lucy-Ann appeared behind her. "Back, you two!" she ordered.

"Oh, *Mum!*" wailed Dinah.

"Well, two minutes then – then straight back to bed," Alison said, and stalked off.

The girls went into the cabin. "What's going on?" said Dinah.

"Sshh! Keep your voice down. Mum's on the warpath. Kiki broke the bottle."

"Oh – what a shame," said Lucy-Ann. "Bad Kiki!"

"Poor Kiki! Poor Kiki!" the parrot corrected her indignantly.

"I'll see if there's a dustpan and brush in Ingrid's cupboard," said Philip. "We'd better get this lot cleared up before someone cuts themselves." He walked out.

Dinah picked up the ship from the floor and examined it. "Oh, dear," she said. "It's got a split in its side."

"Maybe I can fix it," said Jack. "Let me see."

"Hang on," said Dinah. "There's something inside it... I can't get it out—"

"Let me see!" insisted Jack. Dinah passed it to him and he began to probe gently with his forefinger. "It's no good. Too tight. Pass me those tweezers."

Dinah passed them to him and, very carefully, he inserted them into the split in the galley's side. "I've got hold of it!" he said. "Now I've just got to get it out..."

Meanwhile, Philip had discovered a dustpan in Ingrid's large cupboard next door. He'd also discovered Igor's hiding place. But he was completely oblivious to this second discovery because Igor's disguise was so good. Whistling, Philip left the cupboard, shutting the door behind him.

"It's not my night," groaned Igor, as he pulled a large plastic bucket off his head and pushed away a wet mop. Then he eased his way over to the wall adjoining the boys' cabin, pressed a glass to his ear, and began to listen.

"It's coming!" said Jack eagerly.

"What's coming?" asked Philip,

walking in.

"Don't know yet," said Dinah.

"I think it's a bit of paper," said Jack, frowning with concentration. "There!"

Triumphantly, he held up a piece of parchment. Everyone gathered round him to examine it. It was some kind of painting. The parchment was yellow with age, cracked and torn round the edges, but the paint seemed to glow in the dark cabin.

"*Wow*," breathed Philip. "What *is* it?"

The parchment was divided unevenly into four, with a strange interwoven symbol in the centre. In each of the four squares there was runic writing. The first square showed a coastline, an ancient pillar with a cross, and the drawing of a footprint with six lines above it and five alongside. The second square showed a smiling woman wearing a crown, surrounded by coins. The third square looked creepy. It was a great-eyed snake floating over the head of a monk. Then in the last square, there was a boat.

"That's *your* boat, Jack!" cried Philip, excitedly.

"Yes, and that must be Princess Andrea," said Lucy-Ann, pointing.

"It's a map of some kind," added Dinah.

"It must be coded instructions," breathed Jack.

"Are you guys thinking what I'm thinking?" said Philip.

And together, the four shouted, "*TREASURE!*"

CHAPTER EIGHT

On the other side of the wall, Igor was nearly bowled backwards by the sudden loud shout from the children. Hastily he pulled out his mobile phone and tapped in a number.

"Hi, Boss, it's me," he said into the mouthpiece. "It's definitely the one."

At the other end of the line, Slade gripped his phone fiercely. "How do you know?"

Igor swallowed painfully. "Because, Boss – the kids have found the map."

"They what??!!"

"It was an accident, Boss, honest."

Slade took a deep breath. His henchman may have strong muscles, but his *brain!* –

"OK, stay there," he rapped. "I'm on my way, as soon as I can organise some help."

"Help?" queried Igor. What did his boss

need help for? He had him!

"Yes," hissed Slade. "And I know just who to use for this one!"

The children were up early the next morning, far earlier than Igor. He was snoozing under a rather damp tarpaulin in a lifeboat.

As soon as they were dressed, Dinah and Lucy-Ann went along to the boys' cabin to have a look at the treasure map by daylight.

"I wonder where that coastline is," said Philip, thoughtfully.

"Could be anywhere," replied Dinah. "Could be somewhere around here!"

"Well, exactly – we could be sailing right past it."

"Or it could be in the Mediterranean—" put in Jack.

"Or the Shetlands—" added Lucy-Ann.

"Or the Aegean Sea!" finished Dinah.

"Wherever it is, let's have a go at finding it!" cried Philip.

"Yeah!" shouted Jack and the girls.

Kiki screeched happily and flapped away from Jack's shoulder to land on the chest of drawers.

"What we should do is show the map to

Ingrid," said Lucy-Ann, laughing. "That runic writing is just the same as the *Andrea* on the boat."

"Good idea," said Jack. "After breakfast. Come on, hurry up or there won't be any cornflakes left."

"*Cornflakes*—" started Dinah scathingly; then she broke off. "Hey, do you hear that?" There was a distant whirring sound, growing louder.

"Sounds like a helicopter."

"Perhaps it's landing someone on board."

"They must be pretty important to have their own helicopter," said Philip. "Come on – let's go and see!"

The noise of the chopper woke Igor in his lifeboat bed. "Hi, Boss!" he called out blearily, waving one huge hand.

The four children stood and stared as the helicopter landed on deck and Slade and a boy of about Philip's age got out. As he passed, the boy gave a half-smile in their direction. The children watched as the man and the boy were escorted downstairs to their cabins, with two stewards following behind to carry all the luggage they had brought. Then the four of them hurried off to the dining room. They were famished!

"OK, let's go through this one more time," Slade was saying to the morose-looking boy in front of him. "All right, who am—" He paused as he lunged forward, grabbed the boy's Gameboy and tossed it on the bed. "Who am I?"

"You are Marek Epilenska," muttered the boy sullenly, "known to your friends as Eppy–" He caught a threatening glare from Slade, and injected a little more enthusiasm into his voice as he went on: "You're a watch manufacturer."

"Put a smile on your face," complained Slade. "Remember what I'm doing for you. OK, who are you?"

"I am Lucas Epilenska, your son," said the boy with forced brightness. "I am fourteen years old. I was born in Paris. My mother Arianna can't be with us because she's on a business trip and –"

"That's good, that's good. Now, don't forget it. And take that gum out of your mouth! You're supposed to be the son of a respectable businessman."

Glowering, Lucas pulled the gum from

58

his mouth and deposited it in a nearby ashtray. Slade leant forward, snatched off Lucas's hat and jammed it on again, back to front.

"That's better," he said. "Now – let's go and play happy families!"

Alison and the children were just finishing a huge breakfast when Slade and Lucas walked through the door. Philip immediately nudged Dinah, who nudged Jack, who laughed, spilt his drink, and nudged Lucy-Ann.

"All right, you lot," said Alison. "What's the big secret?"

"They're the people the helicopter brought," explained Lucy-Ann.

"The man looks really creepy," muttered Jack.

"Jack! Really!" remonstrated Alison, as she stood up to go.

As the five made their way to the door, Slade spun round and flashed his most sincere smile in their direction.

"Hi!" he said warmly. "The name's Marek Epilenska, and this is my son, Lucas."

"Oh – hello! I'm Allie Mannering, and this is Dinah, Philip, Lucy-Ann and Jack.

Pleased to meet you, Mr – er –
Epi..len..ska."

"Hey – call me Eppy. All my friends do."
And Slade smiled again. "Care to join us
for a coffee?"

Alison smiled back. What a charming
man, she thought. "I'd love to," she
replied.

"Another reason we decided to come,"
Slade was saying genially, as they all sat
together in the dining room, "is that it's
Lucas's birthday next week. Unfortunately
my wife couldn't come."

"Really?" said Dinah. "That's a
coincidence! It was Jack's birthday
yesterday!"

"No kidding! Hey, we missed Jack's
birthday by one day, Lucas."

"Did you get some good presents?"
asked Lucas, politely.

"Yes thanks," said Jack.

"I gave him a ship in a bottle," piped up
Lucy-Ann. "But the bottle broke—"

Quickly, Jack nudged his sister's back.
He didn't want her to give too much away.

"It broke? How terrible!" said Slade.
"Was the ship damaged?"

60

"No, the ship's fine," replied Jack.

"Lucas, you said you had some shopping to do," said Slade. "Hey – would you kids show him where the shop is?"

"Sure," said Dinah, getting to her feet. "Let's go."

As the five children trooped out, Slade leaned confidentially over to Alison. "Great kids you've got there," he said.

"Oh, thank you," replied Alison. He really *is* a charming man, she thought, as they continued to chat, and she told him about their life at Craggy Tops with Uncle Joss.

CHAPTER NINE

Below deck, Ingrid was on her cleaning round. She unlocked the door to the boys' cabin and walked in.

"Hi, Kiki! Only me!"

Kiki liked Ingrid – mainly because she often saved her special scraps from the dining room! Kiki flapped about cackling happily as Ingrid made the beds and tidied round; then squawked warningly as Ingrid picked up the model boat and dusted it.

"All right, Kiki, I'm not going to damage it. How do you like the cruise?"

Kiki hopped from foot to foot.

"Maybe you need a change of scene, ay?"

As though she understood, Kiki flew onto Ingrid's shoulder.

"Come on," said Ingrid, laughing, "you can come with me to Dinah and Lucy-Ann's cabin."

Once there, Ingrid had only just started to clean when there was an announcement over the Tannoy system:

"Attention all A-deck stewards. Please report to the purser's office immediately."

"Hear that, Kiki?" grumbled Ingrid. "It's always something. You stay here, and I'll be right back."

Then she went out, locking the door behind her.

Grunting to himself, Igor made his way stealthily along the corridor, looking for the boys' cabin.

"Now which one was it?" he wondered. Memory wasn't one of his strong points. Stopping outside the girls' cabin, he knocked cautiously. He slowly turned the doorknob, but it was locked. Angrily, he rattled it.

"Naughty banana! Naughty banana!" came a shrill voice from inside.

Alarmed, Igor shambled away!

"Come on, everybody choose one!" Lucas was saying, as the kids looked through a rack of T-shirts. "Dad won't mind."

Dinah glanced at Philip, eyebrows

63

raised. Their new friend was generous to a fault! "Are you sure?" she asked.

"Yeah. Oh – and Jack – I have something else for you as well." Lucas pulled out a flashy-looking digital watch, all dials and buttons. "It's one of the ones my dad sells. Happy birthday for yesterday."

"Wow," said Jack, his eyes lighting up. *"Thanks!"*

"Hang on – I'll just set the time," said Lucas, and he started pressing buttons.

"Good job Lucas is doing it for you," said Lucy-Ann. "It looks very complicated."

"Not really," replied Lucas. "There!" He handed the watch to Jack, who eagerly put it on.

On the deck, Slade was pacing anxiously. Then from his pocket he drew out a slim radio tracking device and smiled as he saw the winking light. Swivelling it round, he followed the direction of the pointing arrow – right into the path of the five children. Grinning, he ducked out of sight. Lucas had done his job! Now to switch into the sound –

BLAAAAAGH!

A foghorn overhead nearly deafened Slade. He clamped his hands to his ringing ears. Drat! Had he lost them?

"*Pssst!*"

What *now*? Slade swung round, irritated, to see Igor's huge head peeking out from a lifeboat. "Have you got the map?" he asked eagerly.

"Ah, Boss! There was someone in there, Boss!"

"There couldn't have been!" snapped Slade. "They were all with Lucas!"

"No, no – I heard them! They called me a – a naughty banana."

"*What?!*" Slade rolled his eyes heavenward. "You fool – that was their *parrot!*"

"Parrot?"

"Parrot! Now get back down there and find that map!"

"Yes, Boss."

"Break down the door if you have to!"

"Sure, Boss," Igor chuckled. Breaking down doors was something he was good at!

"*Snap!*"

Lucy-Ann and Lucas were playing cards in the sun lounge, while the other three chatted.

65

"So what do you think of him?" said Philip quietly, nodding at their new friend.

"Seems OK to me," replied Dinah. "What do you think, Jack?"

Jack shrugged. "I suppose he's all right. He's sticking around us a bit though, and we need to get that map translated."

"Why don't we just slip away now and show the map to Ingrid?" Dinah suggested. "She's usually doing our cabins about this time."

The three stood up, but before they could get very far Lucas called out, "Hey! Where are you guys going?"

"Oh – just for a walk on the deck," said Dinah.

"Hang on – we'll come!" said Lucas brightly, getting to his feet.

Philip forced a smile. Still no escape!

Below deck, Ingrid had returned to the girls' cabin. Kiki was very pleased to see her.

"Back to work, ay, Kiki?" sighed Ingrid, as she started picking up clothes. Those kids were great – but not exactly tidy!

Outside the door, Igor had come to a halt. He still wasn't sure which cabin was the right one. Oh, well. Fixing his eyes on the girls' cabin door, he squared his massive shoulders and prepared to charge. Then from inside the cabin he heard the shrill command: "Wipe your feet! Wipe your feet!"

Igor was used to obeying simple commands. He wiped his feet immediately!

From inside, Ingrid heard the scraping noise and looked up. "Do you hear someone, Kiki?" she said. And, just as Igor began his bull-like charge, she opened the cabin door. Unable to stop, Igor hurtled in and landed with a crash on the nearest bed.

"What on earth are you *doing*?" Ingrid gasped.

"Naughty boy! Naughty boy!" shrieked Kiki.

"Er... sorry," mumbled Igor, rubbing his head where it had made hard contact with the wall. "Wrong cabin." He got to his feet. "Hope I didn't disturb you."

"Now just a *minute*—" began Ingrid, but Igor had put his finger to his lips and disappeared.

Shaking her head, Ingrid turned back to her cleaning. "I tell you, Kiki," she muttered, "you get strange people on cruises."

Very occasionally, Igor's brain worked properly. He'd had time to realise that the cabin he'd hurtled into had not had the model ship in it. Therefore it was the wrong cabin and the *right* cabin must be that one, over there! And here – lying conveniently on Ingrid's trolley on a pile of clean towels – was a bunch of housekeeping keys.

He chuckled gloatingly as he picked up the keys, unlocked the boys' cabin door and stepped inside. Then he tossed the keys back onto the trolley and raised his fist in victory. A perfect shot!

He shut the door quietly and crept into the room. There, on the table, was the model ship. Finally, he'd tracked it down. And this ship had to be the right one, because it was the last one left. He seized it, and tore the side panel off. *There was no map inside!*

Igor collapsed forward, his head in his hands.

CHAPTER TEN

Back on deck, Lucas was still playing the part of the perfect friend. The trouble was, he seemed to enjoy Jack, Dinah, Philip and Lucy-Ann's company so completely that he was impossible to shake off!

"Who'd like a drink and something to eat?" he asked cheerfully, as they passed the ship's coffee bar.

"Yes, please!" said Jack. This was his automatic response to an offer of food.

Philip turned to him. "Weren't you going to feed your bird?" he said pointedly.

"What?"

"Down in the *cabin*," said Philip, even more pointedly.

"Oh! Right. Yes – yes I was."

"I'll come with you," said Dinah, and the two hurried off.

"You have a bird? That'll be interesting," said Lucas, going to follow them, but Philip barred his way. Philip played prop forward at school, and if he barred your way there was no way round it.

"No," he said firmly. "You're buying the food."

"Chocolate milkshake for me, please!" called Lucy-Ann; and Lucas had no choice but to join the queue at the counter.

Dinah and Jack found Ingrid just as she was leaving the girls' cabin with Kiki on her shoulder, and showed her the map.

She stared at it for a while, then she shook her head. "It's very old writing, like on the boat – but it's much more difficult."

"Why?" asked Dinah, disappointed.

"Because they used it over a thousand years ago."

They all studied the map again. They didn't see Igor peering through the door at them.

"No – I've no idea what these words say," announced Ingrid, finally. "Sorry."

"Oh, well," said Jack. "Thanks, Ingrid."

"By the way," Ingrid said, as they were leaving the cabin, "do you two know a very big man with an ugly face?"

Outside the door, Igor's face crumpled. He *wasn't* ugly!

"No – why?" asked Jack.

"He came crashing in here a few minutes ago – it was weird. Said he'd made a mistake."

"He probably had," Dinah assured her, as the two left the cabin. Then she whispered to Jack: "What do you reckon? Sounds like your mystery man again?"

Jack frowned uneasily. "We'd better get back to the others."

"They're taking their time," said Lucas, as he sucked up the last of his milkshake. "I'll go and find them."

"No, no – they'll be back," said Philip firmly. "Look – here they are."

"How's Kiki?" called out Lucas.

Immediately, Jack felt suspicious. "I don't remember telling you her name," he said.

"Oh – it must have been your mum then," put in Lucas quickly. "Anyway, we've had our drinks. We thought we'd go and play cards in the lounge."

"Coming?" said Lucy-Ann.

"You go," said Jack. "I think I'll just stay here for a while."

When they'd gone, Jack glanced around to check no one was looking, and pulled the map out of his pocket. Then he settled down to study it intently. What could the connection between the four strange pictures be? He was too engrossed to notice a huge shadow fall over him from the window outside.

"AAAAAAAGH!!!"

With a terrible roar of triumph, Igor slammed both huge hands onto the glass, just centimetres from Jack's face.

He'd seen the map at last!

Terrified, Jack shot to his feet and made a run for it. Igor charged into the coffee bar like an enraged bear, barging into customers as he lunged at Jack.

"Sir!" remonstrated a steward, but Igor knocked him aside like a rag doll and blundered after Jack.

Heart hammering, Jack raced along the empty deck. He darted through a metal-bar gate and slammed it back just in time for it to crash into Igor's stomach – but it didn't stop the huge man. Jack felt as though nothing would! He clambered up some steel steps and Igor thundered after him, swiping at his legs from below. Jack raced on, up, up, as far as he could go, onto a stretch of deck – and stopped. There was no exit.

Threateningly, Igor closed in on him. "Give me the map!" he growled.

Jack held it tightly behind his back. "No! It's not yours! Leave me alone!"

"It's not yours either," shouted Igor, lunging at Jack. Suddenly a third figure erupted from the side, knocking Igor backwards, and pinning his arms to his sides.

It was Slade!

"It's OK, Jack," he yelled. "I'll handle this now!"

Jack didn't stop to ask questions. Gratefully, he shot down the stairs to freedom.

"Boss!" groaned Igor. "I nearly had him!"

"You *idiot*!" hissed Slade. "You think I want the police crawling all over the ship?"

"But *Boss*—"

"Quiet! Just do exactly as I say!"

CHAPTER ELEVEN

A little over an hour later, Igor was led in handcuffs off the *Aratika* and onto a waiting police launch. The children stood at the rails watching as he went. They were all shaken by what had just happened – particularly Jack.

"Do you think we should tell Mum?" said Dinah.

"No more adventure if we do," answered Philip.

Then Slade and Lucas appeared beside them.

"Jack, you OK?" said Slade, all concern.

"Fine, thanks, Eppy. Thanks for rescuing me like that! Who was he?"

"Just some weird stowaway, I guess. What was that piece of paper he was after?"

There was an awkward pause. Jack glanced quickly at Philip and said, "Oh, just something we found in that model ship that got broken."

Slade shrugged and said, very casually, "Can I have a look at it?"

"It... it's nothing," said Jack, stalling. "It doesn't make sense."

"Maybe I could make some sense of it."

Slowly, unsure, Jack started to pull the precious map out of his pocket. Slade leaned forward. Then –

"There you are!" It was Alison. "I was wondering what had happened to you! What's all the commotion about?"

"Eppy caught a stowaway," announced Lucy-Ann.

Alison turned to Slade, impressed. "Really? You caught a stowaway?"

"Please," said Slade, modestly. "I just raised the alarm, that's all."

"What's that you've got, Mum?" Alison was holding a piece of fax paper in her hand.

"It's bad news, I'm afraid. Uncle Joss has had an accident. We've got to fly back."

"Oh *no*," said Philip. "Poor Uncle Joss!"

"What happened?" asked Dinah. "Is he bad?"

Amid a flurry of concerned questions,

Alison led the children to their cabins. Nobody noticed Slade smiling to himself as he watched them go.

"I've never heard of the nursing home that sent the fax," Alison was saying. "They say Uncle Joss has broken his hip."

"Can't you speak to him?" asked Philip.

"Every time I phone, they say he's asleep. I can't contact Bill. And the line at home is out of order. It's all very—"

Suddenly there was a quick knock, and Slade popped his head round the door.

"Hi, Eppy!" said Alison.

"I've been thinking," said Slade. "Why don't you leave the kids with us for a couple of days while you find out how Uncle Joss is? If it's serious, they can fly back. If it isn't – *you* come back."

"Oh..." began Alison. "That's very kind of you, but—"

"Please, Mum!" begged Philip.

"Yes, go on, Mum," said Dinah, as she raised her camera and snapped Slade's smiling face. "That's a great idea."

But Alison still looked doubtful.

"Oh, come on," said Slade, persuasively. "What could *possibly* happen to them?"

And he smiled steadily at Alison.

"Oh – you're right," she answered.

Early the next morning, the *Aratika* pulled into Anders Isle Harbour. Alison was just finishing packing for her flight back to see Uncle Joss.

"Make sure you do everything Eppy tells you," Alison said. "It's very kind of him to look after you like this."

There was a general chorus of "Yes, Mum".

Ingrid came through the door and announced, "Your taxi for the airport is here, Madam."

Alison turned to her. "Oh, Ingrid. I hate rushing off like this. You will keep an eye on them for me, won't you?"

" 'Course I will," Ingrid assured her.

"Now, no running off and getting into trouble, right?" Alison said.

"No, Aunt Allie" said Jack. He kissed her on the cheek and sailed past, Kiki on his shoulder.

"Jack?" said Alison. "What's he up to? Oh – come on, you lot." Picking up her handbag, she shepherded the three down the gangplank towards the waiting taxi.

"Now, I'll either see you in two days or I'll make arrangements for you to come home," Alison said as the taxi driver loaded her bags into the boot. "Take care of yourselves and say goodbye to Jack for me."

"And you say hello to Uncle Joss for us," added Philip.

"Smile!" said Dinah, aiming her camera. "Oh, drat – the film's run out."

Alison smiled anyway as she got into the taxi. "Goodbye!" she called.

Lounging at the ship's rails, Slade and Lucas watched Alison and the children saying their goodbyes. Surreptitiously, Slade slipped a small packet into Lucas's hand. "Here. Bug their cabins while they're empty. *Prontolo!*"

Lucas scurried off.

In the boys' cabin, Lucas found the perfect place for his listening bug – under the shade of the table lamp. Smirking, he left to bug the girls' room in the same place.

CHAPTER TWELVE

As soon as they'd waved off Alison, Philip and the girls set off to track down Jack. This was always an easy job when Jack had Kiki with him – you just followed the squawks.

They discovered him seated at a table in the library, surrounded by his portable computer, his scanner and a huge atlas. Kiki was on his shoulder, nibbling gently at his ear.

"What are you doing?" asked Lucy-Ann, as they sat down next to him.

"I've scanned the map into my computer – look."

They craned to look at the PC screen. Sure enough, there was the coastline and the cross, the strange, glowing colours of the map perfectly copied. Jack had scanned the map into the computer in its separate quarters. He flicked from the coastline to the smiling princess, then to the snake hovering over the monk, and last of all he called up the ship itself. It was odd to see such ancient drawings on a computer screen.

"And now," said Jack, "I'm putting in every coastline from the Shetlands to the Suez from this atlas."

"And?" prompted Dinah.

"And the computer works out if any of the coastlines from the atlas matches the shape from the treasure map."

"Brilliant!" breathed Philip.

"Hi – what are you doing?"

The children looked up, annoyed. Lucas had tracked them down yet again. Philip hastily snatched the treasure map up from the table and shoved it in his pocket.

"Hi," said Dinah, unenthusiastically.

"Neat computer," said Lucas, joining them. "I wish I had one like that."

The computer beeped urgently.

"What's it doing? asked Lucas, craning round to see the screen.

Jack shrugged. "Oh, just my school geography project—"

A flashing message appeared on the

screen: *MATCH FOUND. PRESS ENTER.*

"– but I've had enough now." Jack reached quickly to switch it off.

But Lucas was quicker. He leant over and pressed ENTER, saying, "Hang on – you'll lose the data if you switch it off now."

ANDERS ISLE and some statistics came up on the screen. Jack pushed Lucas's arm away and switched the computer off.

"Anders Isle?" said Lucas. "That's where we are now, isn't it?"

Dinah glared at Lucas. The atmosphere around the table, already tense, fairly crackled.

"Is it?" said Jack, irritably. "I wouldn't know."

"Oh, yes, I'm sure—" babbled Lucas.

Philip stood up.

"Goodbye! Goodbye!" shrilled Kiki – and Lucas left.

"I wish he'd leave us alone!" exploded Jack, as the door closed. He switched the computer on again, tapped in an entry, and a map of Anders Isle appeared on the screen.

"So – the cross marks the spot," said Philip.

"Brilliant," said Lucy Ann. "Maybe we should ask Eppy to take us there."

"Maybe," pondered Philip. "But we still don't know what the runic writing means. Let's keep it a secret for now."

Just then, Ingrid walked into the library with a vase full of beautiful flowers. "What are you lot doing in here?" she said. "You should be outside in the fresh air."

"We're reading about Anders Isle," explained Dinah.

"Are you? I have a friend here who knows everything there is to know about Anders Isle. He's a priest – and he's also a bit of a scholar. He'd probably be able to help you with the writing on that old map of yours, too."

"Oh, really?" said Philip eagerly. "Would he see us?"

"I'm sure he would." Ingrid took pen and pad from her pocket and started scribbling. "His name's Owen Tournet. Here's his address. He lives just outside the port."

"Thanks, Ingrid!" cried Lucy-Ann.

"Don't mention it," said Ingrid, turning to go. "And give him my regards."

"Wow!" enthused Philip. "This guy

could probably put the whole thing together for us!"

Down in Slade's luxury suite, Lucas was fiddling with the aerial of a radio transmitter.

"The bugs are working, then?" said Slade. "You sure?"

"Yes," replied Lucas. "Now what?"

"Whatever's on that map, they need to get it translated. So we just wait and watch them a little bit longer. And listen."

"And then can I go home?"

"All in good time, my boy. All in good time."

Lucas subsided miserably.

"They're bright kids, though," went on Slade. "If I'm not mistaken, they'll be giving us the slip. And when they do –"

"What?"

"– we'll just set our bloodhound on them!"

Later that day Slade's "bloodhound" was lurking behind a bush on a country road, with the tracker that was linked to Jack's watch in his hand. He was wearing a bright pink cycling helmet and he looked even uglier than usual.

Igor had followed the children out of the port to a cycle hire shop, where Philip and Jack had moaned bitterly about there only being pink helmets left. Igor had chuckled over this until it dawned on him that he'd have to wear one, too. His face had grown even longer when he realised there were only child-sized bikes left to hire. But his boss had said follow the children, and that was what he was determined to do.

Igor looked up with a start as the four children suddenly went speeding by on their hired cycles. Hastily, he mounted his bike and followed them, wobbling wildly.

After five minutes' uncomfortable riding, he'd reached a sign showing the way to Andersea Port. He clambered off his bike, and, with much groaning and heaving, twisted the sign so that it pointed in the wrong direction. That would fool those brats! Then, chuckling proudly, he rode on after them once more.

CHAPTER THIRTEEN

Back in London, Bill was growing impatient. He strode into Sir George Houghton's office, and demanded, "Still no news on the missing galley, sir?"

Sir George put down his cup of tea, and picked up a document. "As a matter of fact, there is. We've found a reference in a twelfth-century chronicle. Saint Bragwaine writes: "Y strangge shyppe in y nighte perted –"

Bill coughed. "And – er – in modern English, sir?"

"A model galley recorded in the goods and chattels of an obscure monastic sect in the Channel Islands." He looked up at Bill. "Isn't that where Allie and the children have gone?"

"Well, yes – as a matter of fact, it is."

"Then why don't you go down there and check this out? And see Allie at the same time?"

Bill smiled in surprise – and delight. "That's very kind of you, sir! I'll just send a fax."

And he hurried off.

After an hour's cycling, Philip, Dinah, Lucy-Ann and Jack arrived safely at Owen Tournet's house, and were having tea in his delightful, flower-filled garden.

"Mmm, delicious," enthused Dinah, taking a large bite out of an almond slice.

"Good. Tuck in," said Owen.

"It's nice of you to see us like this," said Philip.

"Not at all. Any friend of Ingrid is a friend of mine. Now – what is it you want to show me?"

Jack picked up his PC and tapped in a command. The picture of the monk and the snake came up on the screen. "Could you tell us what the words mean?" he asked.

Owen adjusted his glasses, and concentrated on the screen. "This is very interesting. It says: The guardian will show the way."

A few more taps from Jack, and the picture of the princess was displayed.

"Hmm. It says: Beware of the smiling princess."

Next, Jack called up the picture of the ship.

"This says: Turn the ship north."

"What do these two symbols above the ship mean?" asked Philip.

"That's the figure seven, and that's five. I wonder what it all means?"

Hurriedly, Jack pulled the computer away and shut it down. He hadn't shown Owen the picture of the coastline. How could they be sure they could trust him – or anyone?

Owen smiled understandingly. "You don't have to tell me if you don't want to. But can I see the princess again?"

Jack put the PC back on the table, and tapped in a command. The princess materialised on the screen.

"If you find one of these coins, hold on to it," said Owen, pointing to the coins sketched in behind the writing. "One of them just sold at Sotheby's – for *fifty thousand pounds*."

"Philip, are you sure this is the right way back?" shouted Dinah, as the four raced along on their bikes after saying goodbye to Owen.

"You saw the sign," snapped Philip. "This is the way to Andersea Port."

Igor was lying in wait behind a tree. Literally lying, because he was fast asleep and snoring, oblivious to the bleeping of his tracker.

"But the road didn't look like this on the way here..." complained Lucy-Ann.

"No, it didn't," agreed Jack. "Look – this is a dead end. Come on, let's turn back."

And as the children wheeled round, Igor woke with a start and staggered to his feet.

"You're going *NOWHERE!*" he roared, rushing at them, huge arms outstretched to grab.

Lucy-Ann screamed as they all swerved, desperately trying to dodge him.

"Give me the *MAP*," he bellowed.

"He's the stowaway from the ship!" yelled Jack.

"Split up!" shouted Philip. "Meet us in town – come on, Jack, *move!*"

"I'm coming!"

Igor growled in fury as he saw the children veering off in different directions. He grabbed his bike and mounted it.

"Quick – duck down here!" shouted Philip, and the two boys skidded at top speed down a steep slope.

Igor followed them even faster, too fast to see the gnarled tree root jutting out of the ground. He smashed into it, and his wheel buckled crazily. Then poor Igor completely lost control of his bike, hurtled off it, flew into the air – and hit the side of a tree trunk!

Philip and Jack burst into loud laughter at the sight of their attacker, sitting in a bruised and groaning heap on the ground.

Igor didn't like being laughed at. "That's not funny!" he wailed, as the boys grabbed their bikes and sped off.

In his cabin, Slade was growing impatient. "Where's Igor?" he snarled. "He's been gone for—"

He broke off as he heard muffled noises through the radio transmitter. "It's those *kids*!" he spat. "What are they doing back in their cabins?"

"But we saw him being led away in handcuffs!" he heard Lucy-Ann say.

"Maybe the police just gave him a warning," said Jack.

"Well, anyway, what do we tell Eppy?" asked Dinah.

"We'll just tell him we got lost," said Philip. "Now I'm going to get changed. I'm filthy!" And he and Jack went next door to their cabin.

Kiki was overjoyed to see them. Screeching, she launched herself so enthusiastically at Jack that she knocked the table lamp over.

"What's going on?" muttered Slade. The radio transmitter had suddenly gone dead. He held it close to his ear – and jumped back in pain as Kiki gave another high-voltage shriek!

"Kiki, I'm sorry," Jack was saying soothingly. "We came back as soon as we could."

"What's all the noise about?" asked Dinah, as the girls appeared at the doorway. "Oh – clumsy elephant! Is the lamp broken?"

"No." Philip stooped to pick up the lamp – and stopped in his tracks. He'd seen the bugging device underneath the shade! "It's – absolutely – *fine*," he said slowly, putting his finger to his lips and then pointing urgently to the bug.

Back in his cabin, Slade was wondering why everything had gone quiet. Philip had handed the lamp to Jack, who had detached the bugging device and was now busy working on it with a screwdriver, attaching a long piece of wire to it. Dinah was writing on a piece of paper. And Lucy-Ann had gone to fetch the lamp from the girls' cabin – and discovered a bug on that, too. Philip smiled, and detached it too from the shade.

Then, with a flourish, Dinah turned with her "script" and gave it to Philip.

"Have-you-done-it-yet?" read Philip, speaking into the bug like a microphone; then he handed the script and bug to Jack.

"Yes," read Jack clearly. "You know the teddy bears in the shop? They haven't sold a single one during the whole cruise. So I've hidden the map in one of them." And he handed the bug to Dinah.

· "Sounds like a good place to me!" read Dinah; then she grinned, walked over to the porthole, and dropped the bug through the gap.

The smile faded from Slade's face when the children's conversation gave way to clatters – and then watery gurgles!

Impatiently, he grabbed a wad of money from his jacket and thrust it at Lucas. "Go!

Go to the shop, boy. Get all those bears. Every single one. Go on! Quick, quick!"

Lucas scarpered.

"Now to find out who's really behind all this," said Jack, as the four sped along to the shop – just in time to see Lucas hand a thick wad of notes to the startled shop assistant, and start scooping up armfuls of bears.

"Lucas!" breathed Lucy-Ann in disbelief.

"Sshh!" warned Philip.

The shop assistant, delighted with the huge sale, hurried to hold a large bag open for Lucas to drop the bears in. Then he left the shop, a bulging bag in either hand. Dinah nodded to Philip, who went one way with Lucy-Ann; then she and Jack dodged along the corridor behind Lucas.

Lucas disappeared into Slade's suite and slammed the door shut. "Here they are!" he announced.

Immediately, Slade fell on the bears and started ripping them open with his penknife, searching inside. Fur and stuffing flew around the room.

"Come on, boy," he snapped. "You too!"

Shrugging, Lucas joined in. Bear after bear hit the wall as the two searched frantically for the map.

Outside, Dinah pressed her ear to the door. "I can't hear a thing!" she whispered.

Grinning, Jack produced his computer, from his pocket, with the wired bug attached. "Follow me!" he murmured.

He crouched down beside an air vent on the outside wall. Then he tapped some instructions into his PC and slowly, carefully, pushed the bugging device through the slats in the air vent – and into Slade's room.

Words began to appear on the PC screen.

THIS IS THE LAST BEAR! ALL EMPTY! ARE YOU SURE YOU GOT THEM ALL?

POSITIVE. I THINK THEY'RE ONTO YOU.

&&%%$$!!

Dinah put her hand over her mouth and giggled. The computer had censored

Slade's last words!

There was a pause. Inside the room, Slade had grabbed the phone and punched in a number. Then the screen spelt out:

IT'S ME. CHANGE OF PLAN. WE'RE GOING AFTER THE SILVER NOW. YOU CAN START BUYING THE GUNS IN FORTY-EIGHT HOURS.

"*Guns!*" breathed Jack. Swiftly, he pulled the bugging device out through the air vent and he and Dinah sped away.

"It's Eppy!" hissed Jack, as they collided with Lucy-Ann and Philip in the doorway to the boys' cabin. "He's behind everything!"

Jack ushered everyone inside and shut the door.

"He wants the treasure to buy guns!" squealed Dinah.

"Are you sure?" said Philip.

"Yes, we heard him," said Jack. "We've got to get away – and we've got to get to the treasure before he does!"

CHAPTER FOURTEEN

It was a race against time. They had to get a good head start on Slade; they had to leave the ship before he realised what they were up to. The boys grabbed their rucksacks and jammed in torches and as much warm clothing as would fit.

"We can hide near town overnight and bike overland tomorrow," Jack said, tucking his compass safely into a side pocket.

"And if they follow us?" asked Philip.

"We'll be OK. They can't cover all the roads."

"Come on then – let's leg it!"

As Jack slung his bag across his back he didn't notice his computer slide out of a side pocket and fall on the bed. The boys raced from the room and down the corridor, Kiki flapping along behind.

*

Dinah and Lucy-Ann had packed their bags and were now frantically grabbing food from the beautifully laid-out buffet table in the dining room.

"Why can't we just tell the police?" wailed Lucy, holding open a bag as Dinah stuffed in bread rolls. "And wait for Bill?"

"Because we're here and he isn't," snapped Dinah.

They raced from the dining room – and screamed. There was Slade, running straight at them. Lucy-Ann slammed the food bag in his stomach, and the girls made their escape, round a corner – slap-bang into Philip and Jack!

"Eppy's chasing us! Eppy's chasing us!" shrieked Dinah. The four turned and hared up some stairs – and there was Igor, a big plaster on his nose and his arm in a sling, blocking the way. He roared at them, grabbing at Philip. Philip barged him off, and just as Igor lunged at Jack, Kiki flew up from behind, screeching. Igor batted the bird away and grabbed at Lucy-Ann as she ran past, seizing hold of her bag. Lucy-Ann let go of the handles and ran on, racing for the gangplank with the other three.

On the quay, they leapt on their bikes. Slade and Lucas rushed to the ship's railings just in time to see them make their escape.

"They're getting away!" cried Lucas.

"Don't worry. We've got the tracker so we'll know exactly where they are."

He turned as Igor shambled up to join them. The big man was peering greedily into the bag full of food he'd snatched from Lucy-Ann.

"Igor! The tracker!"

Igor jumped, retrieved the tracker from his pocket and handed it to Slade. At the edge of the harbour, the four children were just disappearing from view. Slade laughed, and turned on the tracker. It beeped as the arrow remorselessly traced the course of the four fleeing children.

For the first fifteen minutes the children cycled hell for leather, heads down and eyes in front. Then Philip turned sharply, and led them off the main road and along a rough track.

"I'm sure they're not behind us," said Jack, peering over his shoulder.

"So can we slow down?" panted Lucy-Ann.

"No," barked Philip. Then he veered off onto another intersecting lane, and shot through some dense trees. He wasn't taking any chances!

Ten hard-cycled minutes more, and he allowed everyone to slow down. The children couldn't believe their luck. No one seemed to be after them. They couldn't afford to stop, though. They cycled for three long hours that late afternoon, Kiki gripping determinedly onto Jack's handlebars. Occasionally she'd take off for a short flight when the going got too bumpy. Jack made constant reference to the map and his compass, shouting out directions to Philip at the front. Only when it had really got too dark to see would he agree to stop for the night.

"We've gone *miles*," moaned Lucy-Ann. "My legs are going to fall off."

"This looks like a reasonable place to camp," said Dinah, slowing down by a clump of fir trees.

"Yes, it's OK," said Philip, looking around. "Let's stop here."

They pulled up and stacked their bikes against a tree-trunk. At least the ground looked even, and there were soft pine-needles to lie on.

Jack threw his rucksack down. "I'm starving," he announced.

"So what's new?" snapped Lucy-Ann. She was hungry too.

"We'll find something tomorrow," promised Philip.

"We're bound to find some nuts or berries," added Dinah. "Now come on, let's make ourselves as comfortable as we can."

They spread some jumpers on the ground, and huddled up together for warmth. Somewhere in the trees, an owl was hooting. Kiki chirruped nervously to herself as she settled down on a nearby branch.

"Are we in the right place, Jack?" asked Philip.

"I – think so. We'll check the map in the morning when it's light." He looked at his watch. "Ten o'clock."

"If Mum was here, she'd say it was time for bed," said Dinah wistfully, as they settled down together.

Slade, elegant in silk pyjamas, was anticipating a far more comfortable night than the children. He checked the arrow on the screen of the tracker. It had been stationary for the last thirty minutes.

"No, they're not going any further tonight," he said in a satisfied tone. "And –" he tapped a large map open on his knee – "I know exactly where they are. Come on, Lucas – bed."

Igor looked up plaintively. He'd spent the last hour trying to mend one of the teddies that had been ripped apart in the search for the map. It had a plaster on its nose and it bore an odd resemblance to Igor himself. "Can I go to bed too, Boss?" he asked.

"No," snapped Slade. He tossed the tracker onto Igor's lap. *"Watch them!"*

Right at the end of that very long day, Alison arrived back at Craggy Tops. The cab driver carried her bag to the door, and she tipped him, smiling tiredly. Straight to bed for me, she thought. Then I'll go and see Uncle Joss in the nursing home first thing tomorrow.

Alison opened the front door and pushed it shut behind her. Then she stiffened. Was that the television? She thought she saw its flicker through the lounge door – then it all went black again. Holding her breath, she started to walk towards the lounge.

What was that? She could have sworn there was a dark shape flitting past, up the stairs. What was going on? Heart pounding, she stooped and got hold of a walking stick from the hall stand.

As she crept towards the stairs, she saw the lights of the taxi reflecting on the wall, reversing out of the drive. She was really alone now.

Stealthily, gripping the heavy stick, she began to climb the stairs. And from the blackness a man leapt towards her, shouting: "Stop right where you are!"

Alison had to grab the banisters to stop herself falling backwards from fright. Then realisation dawned. "Uncle – Joss?" she said, incredulous.

"Allie!" Uncle Joss answered. He had his World War One helmet on, and he was carrying a rifle. At any other time, she might have laughed. But not now.

Slowly, they both lowered their weapons.

"You nearly scared me to death there,"

Alison said shakily.

"Sorry about that, old girl. I thought you were a burglar! Why are you here?"

"I got an urgent message saying you were in a nursing home." Alison pulled the fax from her pocket and handed it to Uncle Joss.

"Oh?" exclaimed Uncle Joss. "There's nothing the matter with me." He studied the fax. "Provincial Health?" he snorted. "Never heard of them!"

"What about the phone being out of order?" asked Alison.

"Oh, that. Must have been those two young idiots from the phone company, who came around to check all the lines."

"Did they show you any ID?"

"Didn't think to ask them for any." He leant forward and looked closely into Alison's face. "Everything all right, my dear?"

"No, it certainly isn't," retorted Alison. "Right. Come with me."

"Are we going somewhere?"

"Yes. You're driving me back to the airport!"

"*Will do!*" said Uncle Joss, saluting, and he marched down the stairs.

At the front door, Alison pointed to the tin hat still on his head. "Er – Uncle Joss – ?" she began.

"Oh! Right-o, my dear. Better leave the gun too, I suppose."

He propped it by the wall, and they left.

CHAPTER FIFTEEN

Jack woke up the next morning stiff and sore with the sun beating down on him. His sister was still fast asleep next to him under a rather scratchy-looking covering of bracken. He yawned, turned to his rucksack and unearthed a boiled sweet which he started to suck. Better than nothing, I suppose, he thought.

Kiki fluttered down next to him, chirruping in an enquiring sort of way.

"Sorry, Kiki," he said. "You'll have to find your own breakfast."

Dinah sat up and looked around her. "Well, it's a glorious day," she said. "Anyone want some chewing gum?"

"That all you got?" grumbled Philip. "No, thanks."

"Where to now, Jack?" said Lucy-Ann, standing up and brushing bracken off her jeans.

Jack pulled out his compass, and spread the old map on his knee. "We need to head east," he announced. "Let's get the bikes and be off."

They cycled for two long hours that morning. As the track got rougher, their stomachs grew emptier.

"I wish *I* could eat grass," said Lucy Ann, as they passed a donkey chewing contentedly.

Jack pulled up to check the map and the compass. "We'll have to leave the road here," he announced.

There was a general groan. "Are you sure, Jack?" asked Philip. "That map's very old."

"It was accurate enough for the computer," Jack retorted. "We have to go over those hills and down to the coast."

"Hills!" moaned Lucy-Ann. "I'm tired."

"Come on," said Dinah. "Let's hide the bikes in that hedge there and get going."

As soon as Bill's plane landed he took a taxi to Anders Isle harbour. Luckily, the *Aratika* was still in dock. He ran up the gangplank and a friendly steward directed him to Alison's cabin.

Ingrid was in there, changing the linen. "Mrs Mannering left yesterday afternoon, sir," she explained. "It was an emergency."

"She left the children alone?" asked Bill, incredulous.

"Oh, no. Mr Epilenska is looking after them."

"Mr – who?" said Bill. He was beginning to feel uneasy.

"Epilenska. Let's see if the kids are in their cabins," said Ingrid.

But the boys' cabin was empty, and so was the girls'. Frantically, Bill started to search the top of the desk.

"What are you looking for?" asked Ingrid.

"I was hoping they'd left a note," Bill answered. "You say you haven't seen them since yesterday afternoon?"

Ingrid was beginning to get worried now. "I'll check the boys' cabin," she said, and left.

Bill pulled open the desk drawer, and discovered Dinah's photographs that she'd just had developed on board. He fanned them out, looking at the happy record of the first days of the cruise.

"That's odd," said Ingrid, walking back into the room. "Jack's left his PC."

Then she glanced at Bill's face. He was staring in horror at a photo of Leon Slade – a jolly, smiling photo, not at all like the sinister picture he'd been shown by Sir George.

"Who's this?" he rasped.

"Oh, that's Mr Epilenska," said Ingrid. "Wh–what's wrong?"

White-faced, Bill seized Jack's PC and tapped in a command. The coastline appeared on the screen; then the smiling princess.

"Ah – that's the map they showed me," said Ingrid. "They were very excited about it, but I couldn't read the old writing. So I sent them to see an old friend of mine."

"I'd like to have a word with him," said Bill, grimly.

Bill was racing down the gangplank just as Alison was running from her taxi towards the ship.

"Allie!" he called out.

"Bill!" she shouted, flabbergasted. "Where are the children?"

"The kids are in danger," he said, as he

caught her hand, "but I've got a lead. *Taxi!*"

*

The children walked for well over an hour in the middle of the day. They'd found some berries that they had all agreed were safe to eat, but that was all. Lucy-Ann was trailing behind because she had a blister, and Philip and Dinah were comparing notes on how hungry they were.

Kiki was hungry, too – and fed up with being jolted along on Jack's shoulder. Without warning, she took to the air and flew across the trees.

"Kiki!" shouted Jack. "*Kiki* – come back!" He stood still for a moment, but Kiki didn't return. "I'll have to go after her," he said.

"We'll wait here," said Philip, slumping to the ground.

"Won't be long," Jack promised, dumping down his rucksack. Then he ran through the trees, weaving and swerving as he followed Kiki's erratic flight.

There was someone else in the wood. Slade, Igor, Lucas and a couple of hired thugs had driven as far as they could in pursuit of the children, and now they were tracking them on foot, following the signals from the watch on Jack's wrist.

As Jack raced after Kiki, Slade pulled up sharply and glared at the arrow on the tracker. It had suddenly swung through ninety degrees.

"What's going on?" he muttered, swivelling on his heel. "They're going back on themselves. Come on, follow me!"

Kiki had come to roost high in a tree shrieking "Don't be late! Where's Jack? Where's Jack?"

Jack stopped beneath her, and called up, "Come on, Kiki. Come down."

With a flutter of white wings, she was on his shoulder. "Naughty girl," he said fondly, stroking her, then suddenly he froze. He'd heard Slade's voice!

"This way! We must be nearly on top of them."

Jack crouched lower, heart pounding. They *had* been followed, after all! "How do they know where we are, Kiki?" he whispered. Then his watch beeped. "Of *course*," he said. "It's a transmitter!"

Quickly, he undid the strap and held the watch out to Kiki. "Pick it up," he urged her.

She leant forward obediently and took it

in her beak. "Good girl, Kiki – now, *FLY*!"

Slade's eyes widened in disbelief as the arrow on the tracker swivelled wildly.

"Over there!" he shouted. "No – that way! Quick!"

Igor shambled off in the direction Slade was pointing. "There's no one over here, Boss," he called.

"That's strange," said Slade. "They've changed direction again. This way! No – this way! No – over here! Follow me!"

Igor was exhausted. "Over here, over there. This way, that way, this way—"

"You have a problem with that, Igor?" snarled Slade. And he flexed his hand like a scorpion's tail at Igor's throat.

"Huh? No, Boss," muttered Igor.

"Good. Now, come on. This way! No – that way! *Over here*!"

Overhead, Kiki squawked merrily and nearly dropped the watch!

Lucy-Ann had filled the time spent waiting for Jack by rummaging in his backpack. "Look what I've found!" she said, putting them into her own bag. "Wine-gums!"

"Great!" said Philip. But he didn't get a

chance to take one because Jack came hurtling back, shouting, "*Quick*! They've been following us!"

"*What*?"

"That watch Lucas gave me – it had a tracking device in it! I've delayed them – but we've got to go!"

"How have you—" began Dinah.

"No time," panted Jack. "I'll tell you later. *HURRY*!"

Jack might have shaken off one tracking device, but the children had left behind another. As Lucy-Ann snatched up her bag, a couple of wine-gums dropped out and lay in the grass, like bright signals; as the four children ran down the road to the coast, another fell out, and then another.

CHAPTER SIXTEEN

Meanwhile, Kiki was still leading Slade and his henchmen on a wild goose chase – or perhaps wild parrot chase is a better description! From tree to tree she flew, up and down, back and round, while the men swerved and panted beneath her.

"Are you sure that thing's working properly?" groaned Igor.

"Of course it is!" snapped Slade. "Over here!" He glared down at the tracker. Its bleeper was right on their position! Then it went right, then it went left –

Slowly, Slade looked upwards. There was Kiki, watch in her beak, doing a little dance on the branch above them. Two steps to the right: two steps to the left. Then she ducked, bowed prettily, and dropped the watch on their heads.

"Back!" yelled Slade, nearly apoplectic

with rage. "Back the way we came!"

"Oh, Boss!" groaned Igor.

"Naughty boy!" shrilled Kiki.

The children had at last reached the shoreline shown in the map. All they could hear was the sound of the waves breaking on the beach and seagulls crying above their heads.

"I think we've lost them," said Philip, checking once more over his shoulder.

Jack raised his binoculars and scanned the beach in front of them. "There it is!" he said excitedly. "There's the cross!"

Lucy-Ann stretched over to take the binoculars from him. As she did so, the last of the wine-gums fell from her rucksack. "That's it, all right," she said, handing the binoculars to Philip.

"Clever girl! Clever girl!" Kiki swooped from the sky and landed on Jack's arm, nuzzling him affectionately.

"Kiki – you're back!" he cried. "Yes, you *are* a clever girl!"

"Come on, then," said Dinah. "Let's take a closer look."

The cross leaned at a crazy angle in the sand, and was hung with seaweed from when high tides had covered it. Next to it was an old, crumbling column, taller than a man and wide enough to climb inside. Broken pieces of stone lay at its base.

The children found their steps slowing almost involuntarily as they drew nearer. The sun had gone behind the clouds now, and the sea looked grey as it lapped at the shore. There was an ominous atmosphere to the place.

Kiki wasn't fazed, however. She flew perkily off to the column and perched on the edge.

"Well – here's our spot," said Jack.

"Let's have a look at the map," replied Philip.

The four crowded round as Jack opened out the old map.

"What's this foot sign?" said Dinah, pointing. "And these marks? Could they be clues?"

"It's obvious!" retorted Philip. "It's the number of steps to take."

"It looks like six forward and five across," commented Lucy-Ann.

"But what if it's five forward and six across?" put in Jack.

"And is it big steps or little steps?"

added Lucy-Ann.

"Big steps, I should think," said Jack.

"But people were smaller in those days," Dinah reminded him.

"I'll do it," said Jack.

"*I'll* do it," insisted Lucy-Ann, and they both started pacing, counting as they went.

"Those are far too big," called out Philip. "I'll have a go. One, two, three..."

"Me too," said Dinah. "One, two, three—"

"I've found something!" shouted Lucy-Ann, crouching down and scrabbling at the sand.

The three others hurried over to join her. Buried in the sand was a strange, circular slab of rock with runic symbols carved on it. It seemed to be set into a square of rock beneath it.

"Those symbols are on the map, too!" breathed Dinah.

"Turn the ship north," quoted Jack. "Look, the symbol for 'Turn' is the same. But turn what?"

"The whole thing?" suggested Philip. "Here goes!"

Using all his strength, Philip tried to twist the stone, but it didn't budge.

"Try the other way," suggested Jack.

"OK. You help."

Four hands pushed and slowly, slowly, the stone twisted round. For a second or so, there was silence. Then from behind them came a grating, grinding, rumbling noise. Kiki squawked and flew upwards.

"Something's happened in the column!" said Dinah. The four ran over and reached the column just as Kiki returned and swooped down into it – and disappeared!

"Jack, give me a leg-up," ordered Lucy-Ann. "I'll see what's happened."

The others hoisted her up the side of the column. With both hands, she gripped the rim and pulled herself up the last few centimetres. Then she peered down into the centre of the column.

"The bottom's opened up!" she shouted. "There are steps! They lead down. This must be it!"

"There are some footholds here, on the other side," said Philip.

"So what are we waiting for?" said Dinah, and first she, then Philip, then Lucy-Ann and finally Jack clambered up the footholds on the side of the column and disappeared into the darkness below.

CHAPTER SEVENTEEN

"Fan out, fan out," yelled Slade. "We *can't* lose them now!" He ran on, frantically looking from side to side. Lucas and the henchmen staggered in his wake.

"Hey, Boss," Igor chuckled. The huge man had stooped to the ground to examine something. "Look what I got." And he waved a wine-gum under Slade's nose. "There's more, too – look."

"It's a *SWEET*, you *IDIOT*!!" screamed Slade, beside himself with rage. Then the significance of the dropped sweet dawned on him.

"Well *done*, Igor!" he beamed. "Well done! Come on! This way. Come on, Igor! Follow the sweets! This way!"

Inside the column was a flight of worn stone stairs, so dark that the children couldn't see what was at the bottom. They switched on their torches and climbed down gingerly, step by step. At the foot they found themselves in a dark, low-ceilinged cavern. Shadows moved on the walls, looming over them. There was an ancient, brooding feel to the place, as though it had lain still for centuries, waiting.

"Creepy!" muttered Lucy-Ann.

Philip trained his torch across the floor and a mysterious blue–black light flickered back at him. "Don't move!" he hissed. "Water!"

They all shone their torches downwards.

A circular pool filled the floor of the cavern, lapping at its walls. The water looked black, as though it went down for ever. Its surface moved slightly, sending weird, rippling shadows across the cavern ceiling.

"Wow!" muttered Jack. "I don't like the look of that!"

"I wonder how deep it is?" said Lucy-Ann.

"I don't know," breathed Dinah, "and I'm *not* going to find out."

On the other side of the pool was an

arched doorway. It was obviously the only way forward.

"We've got to cross," said Philip. "There must be a way."

The children played their torches all round the cavern, across the rough stone walls. Lucy-Ann's torch beam landed on a skull set into the rock, and she gave a shrill shriek.

Dinah jumped. "Lucy-Ann – *please*! We're spooked enough as it is!"

Next to the skull was a painted fresco of a monk, glimmering in the uncertain light.

"Look!" cried Jack. "It's exactly the same as the one on the map!"

"He's walking on water," said Dinah.

"And there's the snake, next to him. This must be the guardian!" added Philip.

"Owen said the guardian would show the way..." mused Jack. "But how?"

Dinah glanced back up at the fresco on the wall. Then she stared fixedly at the water that almost reached her feet. There, emerging from the pool, was a painting of a snake's head. Its tongue seemed to be pointing at her.

"Walking on water," she muttered to herself. "Well, here goes!" And she stepped forward into the pool.

"*No*, Dinah!" shouted Philip, horrified. "*Stop!*"

But Dinah took a step forward. And another. Everyone watched in amazement as she glided safely across the pool and reached the entrance at the other side.

"How did you *do* that?" gasped Jack.

"Oh!" breathed Lucy-Ann. "It's the snake!"

"You got it!" exclaimed Dinah, turning round triumphantly. "Stepping stones – just below the surface – in the pattern of the snake!"

One by one, Philip, Lucy-Ann and Jack safely crossed the pool. Then the four children took a deep breath and stepped through the archway beyond.

Outside on the beach, Igor had bent down to pick up another wine-gum. Surreptitiously, he popped it into his mouth.

"Look!" shouted Slade. "What's that?"

He pointed to the column.

The children found themselves at the mouth of a long, gloomy tunnel. Even with all four torches trained on it, they couldn't see the end. Huddled together, they started to walk forward. At their feet a little stream of water flowed, draining endlessly into the pool they'd crossed. The walls dripped with damp.

At last they came to a standstill in front of a great wooden door which barred their way. It was broken and rotting, hanging off its hinges. The old iron staves which had once held it together jutted out uselessly. Philip got hold of a large slat of wood and pushed it to the ground. Then one by one, the four clambered through the gap.

"What *is* this place?" breathed Dinah, looking round in awe. They'd stepped into a large cavern, high-ceilinged and spacious. A great cross was suspended at the far end. The walls were crumbling now, and tree roots hung like serpents from the walls, but once it would have been an impressive place.

"This must be where the monks lived," said Jack.

"I wouldn't want to live down here," muttered Lucy. "It's too dark and cold."

"Why would anyone build a place like this underground?" wondered Philip.

"Who knows?" said Jack. "Some religious group maybe – who'd been persecuted and wanted to hide away."

Philip led the others through an ornate archway into a small chapel. The air felt stale and dead, unbreathed for centuries.

"I'm scared," said Lucy-Ann in a small voice.

"There's nothing to be scared of, Lucy-Ann," said Philip firmly. "Those monks or whoever they were – they're long gone."

"More ancient wall paintings," said Dinah, heading over to examine them.

"Hey – look at this!" Jack cried. He stepped through a tiny doorway into a room that seemed to be carved out of solid rock. Philip and Lucy-Ann followed him. In the centre of the room was a marble tomb, with runic letters and symbols of coins painted along its side.

"Just like the signs on the map," whispered Lucy-Ann.

"And look!" said Jack, moving to the end. "Here's the princess, and she's smiling."

Philip stared at the princess. Her smile seemed menacing, gloating. "Didn't the map say beware the smiling prin—" he began.

Suddenly the wall at the side seemed to swing out towards them. It was a door, and it was shutting, fast. As it closed, it revealed a skeleton, slumped on the ground.

Lucy-Ann's scream echoed piercingly round the walls. "We're trapped!" she wailed.

Panic-stricken, Philip and Jack started to bang furiously on the stone door.

"Dinah! *Dinah!*"

"Open the door! *Open it – we're stuck in here!*"

Dinah, on the other side, was engrossed in studying the faded wall painting.

"This monk in a boat," she was saying. "If you look closely at what he's holding – I'm sure it's a boat in a bottle." She turned, wondering why no one had come over to see. Then she saw that a door had closed on the tiny side chapel, and heard the banging, muffled by thick stone.

"Oh, *no!* Philip! Jack! *Lucy-Ann!*" she shouted, and rushed to the stone door, barging it with her shoulder. To her relief and amazement, it swung in effortlessly, and Philip, who'd been charging it from inside, stumbled out.

"Oh, thank *goodness*," cried Lucy-Ann, rushing out and hugging Dinah. "I thought we'd have to stay there for ever—"

"Like he did," finished Jack grimly, nodding towards the sprawling skeleton.

CHAPTER EIGHTEEN

Kiki didn't like dark places. As soon as she'd seen Jack disappear through the arch on the other side of the pool, she'd turned tail and flown back up the column steps. Now she was perched on its rim.

"Boss!" came a shout. "There's that dumb bird of theirs!"

"Smart enough to fool *you* a few times, Igor," snapped Slade.

"Huh – featherbrain," snorted Igor.

Kiki flapped up in the air and flew straight over Igor, dropping a present neatly on his head as she passed.

"*Errgh!*" growled Igor, wiping it off in disgust.

"Wipe your feet!" squawked Kiki triumphantly. "Naughty boy!"

"Come on," yelled Slade. "If their bird's here, then they can't be far." He clambered up the side of the column and peered over the rim.

The princess's tomb was the only room off the ancient chapel. There seemed to be nowhere else where the treasure might be hidden. The children paced about, searching for clues.

Lucy-Ann picked up the edge of an old black cloth draped over the altar, sneezing as the clouds of dust got in her nose. And there, underneath, was a stone statue of the *Andrea*, exactly like Jack's model boat.

"I've *found* it," she called, her eyes wide with excitement. "Look, *look*! It's the ship!"

"The treasure must be behind it – or in it," said Jack, as the three rushed over.

"But how do we get to it?" asked Dinah.

"Turn the ship north," quoted Lucy-Ann. "That's what the map said."

"But how?" said Dinah. "It's not a real ship!"

"No, but if you turn a ship, you use the tiller," suggested Jack.

"Let's have a go, then," said Philip. He grasped the statue's tiller and hauled.

A deep, thrilling rumbling echoed round the chapel. Then with a roaring, grinding noise, the entire altar swung back and revealed a small chamber behind it.

The children's amazement turned to bitter disappointment as they peered into the little stone room.

"It's empty!" wailed Dinah. "We've come all this way for nothing!"

Meanwhile, Slade and his henchmen had negotiated the steps down into the cavern and were standing by the black pool, perplexed. Igor shivered and looked nervously around at the flickering, looming shadows on the wall.

"We'll have to turn back, Boss," he said.

But Slade was shining his torch directly in the water, by the snake's head. He liked snakes. He could just make out the shape of one, glimmering below the surface of the water. He guessed that that was the way across. But just to make sure he was right —

"Igor," he barked. "Get over here!"

Reluctantly, Igor manœuvred his huge bulk next to Slade at the edge of the pool.

"Lead the way!" ordered Slade.

"Looks pretty deep, Boss," Igor groaned.

Slade turned on Igor, flexing his hand at

his neck. Igor flinched. Trapped between a scorpion and a snake!

"OK, OK," he muttered, and approached the edge.

The four children could just squeeze into the empty chamber behind the altar. Disconsolately, they sat on the floor as Jack studied the treasure map once again.

"Someone must have got here before us," said Lucy-Ann, sadly. "That's the only explanation."

"But what about the numbers seven and five?" asked Jack. "We haven't – you know, *used* them yet. They must be still to come."

Philip shrugged. "Could be anything." From above, a drop of water fell on his neck and he shone his torch up at the ceiling. The ceiling was composed of rows of small square stones, each one green with slime and lichen.

"Wait a minute!" said Jack, his eyes following the beam of Philip's torch.

"They're just pieces of stone stuck in the roof," said Philip, dismissively.

"But there must be a reason for them," retorted Jack.

Dinah clapped her hands. "That's what

seven and five are! It's a grid!"

"Dinah, you're brilliant!" said Jack. "We count down seven on one side, and five along the other."

"And push that stone or pull it out," added Philip, excitedly. Then he started to count along the stones. "One – two – three – four – five – six – seven." The stones felt clammy to his touch, and he could feel cobwebs sticking to his fingers.

"OK, now go back," said Lucy-Ann.

"One – two – three – four – five," counted Philip. He pressed hard on the stone he'd reached, and tried to shift it with his fingernails, but it wouldn't budge.

There was a disappointed silence. Then Dinah said, "OK. Now try the other way."

This time Jack reached up to count, in the other direction to Philip. "One – two – three – four – five – six – seven," he said, his voice hoarse with tension. "One – two – three... four ..."

He turned to look at the others. This was it!

"*Five*," he said, and pressed with all his might on the square.

Immediately, the stone loosened and fell to the ground. There was a distant rumbling, growing louder – and then there came a glorious flood of shiny silver coins, streaming endlessly out of the roof and piling up on the floor. The children cheered and clapped and laughed. It was like the best fruit machine in the whole world!

"The *Andrea* treasure!" shrieked Lucy-Ann.

"And *we* found it!" crowed Philip.

"And I am *so* grateful for your help..." hissed a malevolent voice.

As one, the children spun round, to see Slade, grinning, in the doorway.

CHAPTER NINETEEN

Bill and Alison leapt out of the taxi and banged furiously on Owen Tournet's door.

"Let him be in!" prayed Alison, near to tears. She couldn't bear not knowing where the children were – or what was happening to them.

Seconds later, the old priest opened the door. "What on earth—?"

"Forgive us for disturbing you like this, sir," broke in Bill rapidly. "But it's a matter of grave urgency. I understand four children visited you yesterday, friends of Ingrid's?"

"Yes... yes... charming young people, but—"

"And they showed you this?" Bill thrust Jack's PC at Owen.

"Yes, I was able to help them with some translations."

"We think this is where they've gone."
Bill pointed to the map.

"Ah! They didn't show me this bit!"
Owen exclaimed. "That's Anders' Cross,
I'd stake my reputation on it. It's located in
a nature reserve about twenty miles east of
here."

"How do I find it?" asked Bill, urgently.

"I've got an Ordnance Survey map of
the island somewhere—"

"You're a genius," said Bill, with a sigh
of relief.

Minutes later, Bill, Alison and Owen
were studying the map. Then Bill pulled
out his mobile phone and pressed the code
that got him a direct line to Sir George
Houghton.

"Yes, we've located them, sir," he said.
"It's Anders' Cross – grid reference 0234
and 0719. How long will it take the secret
service boys to get there?"

There was a pause, as Bill listened,
frowning. Then he rapped out: "That's too
long, sir. I'm going in by myself."

"No," corrected Alison. "*We're* going
in."

Bill glanced up at her. He never argued
with Alison when she looked that

determined. No one did!

*

"You're *HURTING* me!" wailed Lucy-Ann.

"Let go of her!" shouted Jack.

"Ouch – you little vixen!" This was from Igor! Dinah had aimed a kick at Igor's ankle – and it had made sharp contact!

"Get on with it, get on with it," snarled Slade. "How long does it take you to tie up four brats?"

Igor and the two henchman redoubled their efforts, and soon the children were completely trussed up with rope.

Slade turned to the sack he'd been shovelling the silver coins in, picked a coin up, and kissed it lovingly. "Beautiful condition," he murmured. "And each one worth a fortune!"

He scooped up the last of the coins, and then pushed the four children roughly into the treasure vault.

"What are you going to do with us?" demanded Philip, trying to keep his voice steady.

"Nothing," Slade shrugged. "You're going to stay here."

"For how long?" asked Jack, desperately.

"Until someone finds you," said Slade, with a malicious smile. "Two hundred years, maybe?" And he laughed.

"You're a *murderer*!" shrieked Dinah.

"Clever girl," murmured Slade. "Now – Lucas – leave that sack."

Lucas dropped it numbly. He was very shaken. He knew Slade was cruel but he'd never imagined he could be that evil.

"Tie him up with the others," snapped Slade.

"*What?*" Lucas turned white. "What about our deal?"

"What deal?" asked Slade, slyly.

"You promised me that if I went along with you my father could—"

"Did I?" said Slade, in mock surprise. "Age is a curse! I can't remember saying that!" He turned to Igor and the henchmen. "Now come on – get all this stuff out of here!"

Igor chuckled as he quickly tied a rope round Lucas, pinning his arms to his sides, and manhandled him into the treasure vault with the others.

"Ladies and gentlemen," announced Slade with a flourish, "it's been a pleasure doing business with you." He turned to the stone ship. "And now, if I'm not mistaken, there's the key to the door – Igor?"

"Aaah!" grunted Igor, catching hold of the tiller. "The key!"

"No!" shouted Philip, panic-stricken. *"Don't!"*

But Igor merely laughed, and heaved on the tiller. With a sickening grinding noise, the altar slowly swung back into place, towards the terrified children. They all screamed and cried out, begging to be released, but Slade and the three henchman simply shouldered their sacks and walked away.

Lucy-Ann watched in horror as she saw the edge of the door moving slowly, indomitably inwards. Another few centimetres, and they would be shut in – for ever. Wildly, she looked round for escape – and spotted, at her feet, the stone that had fallen from the roof and released the flood of treasure. She nudged it with her foot into the narrow gap, praying she wouldn't push it too far. The door swung a little further – and stopped, jammed.

"Well *done*, Lucy-Ann!" exclaimed Philip.

"You've saved us!" breathed Dinah.

There was a silence. Then Lucas said, "What now?"

"We've got to get these ropes off," said Jack, suddenly efficient again. "My knife's in my back pocket."

Philip twisted round so that his hands were at Jack's back. Carefully, he eased the fingers of his bound hands into Jack's pocket – and made contact with the cold edge of the knife. It took Philip only a few moments to open it; then he started to saw at Jack's ropes.

Soon, all five children were free. Lucas kept his eyes fixed on the ground, refusing to meet anyone's gaze.

"Right," said Philip determinedly. "Push!"

Everyone knew their lives depended on it: everyone pushed with the last ounce of their strength.

"Push, *push*!" urged Philip again.

"We *are*!" the others groaned.

And then, gradually, grindingly, the altar stone began to move. There was a harsh cracking sound, as if something had snapped in its ancient mechanism, and then it swung slowly open.

"Freedom!" breathed Jack.

Before anyone else could move, Lucas pushed his way past Lucy-Ann and rushed to the door of the chapel.

"Stop, Lucas!" shouted Philip. "Lucas – STOP!"

Lucas ran on. Philip tore after him and tackled him, bringing him to the ground. Then he sat on him so he couldn't move.

"What's the idea?" panted Philip. "What are you doing?"

"I'm going to get him!" spat Lucas furiously. "He lied to me!" And he lurched angrily, trying to shake Philip off.

"You won't stand a chance against those hired thugs of his! You'll get killed!"

"He said he'd stop blackmailing my dad if I helped him." Lucas once more tried to throw Philip off, but Philip didn't budge. "Let me *go*!"

"Not till you calm down."

Lucas knew when he was beaten. "All right," he said, lying still.

"Getting angry won't help. Getting *even* will." And with that, Philip loosened his grip on Lucas and stood up.

Lucy-Ann appeared behind them. "Quick!" she called excitedly. "In here. We've got an idea!"

CHAPTER TWENTY

Kiki hopped slowly down the stone steps, squawking sadly. She didn't like being down in the cavern one bit, but she wanted to find Jack.

Suddenly, Slade appeared at the mouth of the tunnel, at the other side of the pool. He looked back down the tunnel and rapped out: "Igor! Hurry it along!"

Kiki lowered her head and screeched at him, and he jumped, startled.

"Quiet," he snarled, "or you'll be for the pot!"

Carefully, he made his way along the snake's back to the other side of the pool and started up the column steps. Cackling angrily, Kiki flew over his head.

"Boss!" came a plaintive cry from the tunnel. "I think we're going to need a hand here!"

Cursing, Slade returned to the pool. In minutes, he had his henchmen organised, strung out in a human chain through the tunnel and across the pool. They started to toss the sacks of coins one to the other.

"Come on, come on," muttered Slade. "Speed it up." He didn't like the cavern. The watery light from the pool made everything look so eerie.

"Just one left, Boss," called Igor.

And then the most chilling noise split the still air. It was thin, wailing – inhuman.

"What was *that*?" breathed Slade.

Everyone stood still and listened. The wailing came again, a little louder this time, a little more sinister.

"Think it's those kids?" muttered Igor.

"Can't be," said Slade. "They're in there for good." The ghostly noise came again, echoing round the cavern.

"Check it out," ordered Slade. "Move, move!"

Igor pushed one of the henchman ahead of him. There was no way he was going first along that tunnel! "Go, go, *go*!" he said. "I'm right behind you."

Slowly, the men edged into the tunnel, as the wailing seemed to grow louder and more close at hand.

"Find out what's making the noise," snapped Slade. "And if it's that bird – *smash* it!"

Kiki chose that moment to fly straight at Slade's face. He jumped backwards, nearly overbalancing into the pool, put his hand out to steady himself – and recoiled in horror. He'd put his hand straight onto a skull, embedded in the rock!

"Hurry *UP*, you idiots!" he yelled frantically. "Where *ARE* you?"

Suddenly, Igor and the two hired thugs erupted from the tunnel. And behind them, glowing in the half light, was a grinning skeleton, wrapped in a black cloak. Slowly, it raised its bony hand and pointed at Igor, then it made a sudden rush –

With a cry of terror, Igor plunged into the pool, followed by the henchmen. Slade panicked. He turned to grab a sack, meaning to escape, but Kiki landed on it with a bloodcurdling shriek. Furiously, Slade raised his hand to strike.

"Hold it! You're under arrest!"

Slade looked up to see Bill, gun pointing straight at him. Alison stood behind.

"I'll give you half," Slade said,

ingratiatingly.

Bill's frown deepened.

"Three-quarters? Please? Just let me keep *some* of it—"

"Where you're going," said Bill slowly and carefully, "you won't need a penny."

Alison glared at the man who had tricked her, who had endangered her children.

"Oh, you're too harsh, Bill," she mocked. "Why not let him have one bag?"

And, picking up a sack from the floor, she hurled it as hard as she could straight at Slade's chest. He caught it with a great gasp – and toppled over into the black pool below!

"Silly billy! Silly billy!" cackled Kiki in delight.

Across the pool, the skeleton waved happily and dropped its cloak to the ground – to reveal the children. Lucy-Ann's idea had worked brilliantly. They'd taken the skeleton from the Princess's chamber and wrapped it in the cloth from the altar, and that – coupled with some ghostly wailing from Dinah and Lucas – had been enough to scare the villains senseless!

Sir George's secret service men arrived on the scene soon after, and the four wet and dispirited villains were handcuffed and taken off to jail. Lucas was driven away, back to his father, with a promise that the cloud his family had lived under for so long because of Slade's blackmailing would at last be lifted.

Then there was much hugging and kissing between the children and Bill and Alison. Finally, Alison drew back and said, "Well! Now that you're all safe, I've arranged a little surprise."

"What sort of surprise?" asked Bill.

Alison put her arm round his neck and hugged him. "You'll find out," she said.

CHAPTER TWENTY-ONE

The next day was one of those soft September days that seem to hold all the warmth of the summer in them. A wedding party had gathered in Owen Tournet's beautiful garden. His rose bower was the perfect place for a marriage ceremony. And instead of white doves there was Kiki, flapping as romantically as she could from tree to tree.

"I now pronounce you man and wife," Owen announced, beaming happily. "Er – you may kiss the bride."

Eyes shining, Bill bent and kissed Alison – and the children all cheered.

"Now we've got a dad!" said Dinah happily.

"And I've got four wonderful children," said Bill warmly.

Everyone hugged each other. Then

143

Alison drew back and looked serious.

"Right, you lot," she announced. "I've got something to say to you."

"Yes, Mum?" asked Philip. She had her stern face on again, the face no one dared argue with.

"No more adventures. Understood?"

"Yes, Mum," answered Philip obediently. "No more adventures."

"Definitely, no more adventures," added Jack.

"Not a single one," put in Lucy-Ann.

"Wouldn't dream of it!" cried Dinah.

"Definitely," said Lucy-Ann. "Er – not."

Alison frowned at them all jokingly. What were they up to? They weren't usually this compliant.

She couldn't see that behind their backs each and every one had firmly crossed their fingers!

The
Enid Blyton™
Adventure Series

All eight screenplay novelisations from the Channel 5 series are available from bookshops or, to order direct from the publishers, just make a list of the titles you want and send it with your name and address to:

Dept 6,
HarperCollins*Publishers* Ltd,
Westerhill Road,
Bishopbriggs,
Glasgow G64 2QT

Please enclose a cheque or postal order to the value of the cover price (currently £3.50) plus:

UK and BFPO: Add £1 for the first book, and 25p per copy for each additional book ordered.

Overseas and Eire: Add £2.95 service charge. Books will be sent by surface mail, but quotes for airmail dispatch will be given on request.

A 24-hour telephone ordering service is available to Visa and Access card holders on 0141-772 2281.